Kristy and the Kidnapper

Other books by
Ann M. Martin

P.S. Longer Letter Later
(written with Paula Danziger)
Leo the Magnificat
Rachel Parker, Kindergarten Show-off
Eleven Kids, One Summer
Ma and Pa Dracula
Yours Turly, Shirley
Ten Kids, No Pets
Slam Book
Just a Summer Romance
Missing Since Monday
With You and Without You
Me and Katie (the Pest)
Stage Fright
Inside Out
Bummer Summer

THE KIDS IN MS. COLMAN'S CLASS series
BABY-SITTERS LITTLE SISTER series
THE BABY-SITTERS CLUB mysteries
THE BABY-SITTERS CLUB series
CALIFORNIA DIARIES series

Kristy and the Kidnapper

Ann M. Martin

AN
APPLE
PAPERBACK

SCHOLASTIC INC.

New York   Toronto   London   Auckland   Sydney
Mexico City   New Delhi   Hong Kong

ISBN 0-590-52343-0

12 11 10 9 8 7 6 5 4 3 2 1   0 1 2 3 4 5/0

Printed in the U.S.A.   40

First Scholastic printing, April 2000

The author gratefully acknowledges
Ellen Miles
for her help in
preparing this manuscript.

Kristy and the Kidnapper

❋ Chapter 1

"Resolved: We are going to have a blast in D.C.!" Abby threw herself on my bed. "Dibs on the affirmative!" She cracked up. Abby is always cracking herself up.

I have to admit she cracks me up too. She really can be pretty funny. But I guess you'd have to know something about debating to understand why we were laughing.

I'm just learning about it. Debating, that is. We recently finished a unit on it in my English class. It turned out that Abby and I were both pretty good debaters — which is why we were headed to Washington, D.C., for four days. (And why we were getting two days off from school.)

I know, I know. You're probably totally confused. First of all, I haven't even introduced myself.

I'm Kristy Thomas (Kristin Amanda Thomas if you're my mom and you're mad at me). I've spent my whole life — all thirteen years of it — in Stoneybrook, Connecticut, and I'm an eighth-grader at Stoneybrook Middle School, or SMS. I'm a decent student, I guess. I have brown hair and brown eyes and I'm not exactly the tallest person around. That's me.

The girl lying on my bed? That's Abby Stevenson. She's also thirteen and in the eighth grade at SMS. Abby has longish, curly dark hair and beautiful dark eyes. (She wears glasses sometimes and contacts other times.) Her house is down the street from mine, but she hasn't lived in Stoneybrook for nearly as long as I have. She and her twin sister, Anna, (they're identical, but it's easy to tell them apart) and their mom moved here recently from Long Island, in New York. Abby and Anna's dad died in a car accident a few years ago.

Abby and I became friends when she joined this club I belong to, the BSC. That stands for Baby-sitters Club, although it's actually more of a business than a club. Abby's not in the club anymore, but we're still buds.

I am president of the BSC, since the club was my idea.

Not that it's important. Just thought I'd mention it.

Anyway, where was I? Oh, debating.

Debating is a lot like arguing, only you're not supposed to let your emotions rule. Probably the reason Abby and I are both good at it is that we're both sort of opinionated.

"*Sort of* opinionated?" I can hear my best friend, Mary Anne Spier, say.

"That's like saying that van Gogh was *sort of* a good painter." That's what Claudia Kishi, another friend, would probably add.

"Or that Cindy Crawford is *sort of* pretty," I can imagine Stacey McGill — Claudia's best friend — chiming in.

The three of them are in the BSC, and I've known Mary Anne and Claudia forever, so I guess they all know me pretty well. And it's true, Abby and I *are* alike in that way.

Neither of us is shy about saying what she thinks. We both believe in speaking our minds. I think that's a *good* quality, even though once in a while I surprise even myself with the things that pop out of my mouth.

A good debater, according to my English teacher, Mrs. Simon, has to feel comfortable speaking in public. Having the "courage of your convictions" helps too. (That means you're willing to fight for what you believe in.) Only one thing is hard for me in debating: Sometimes you have to stand up for something you *don't* believe in.

I'll explain. In a debate, there are two sides (you knew that). The sides can be individuals or teams of two, three, or four. One side is called the affirmative, the other is called the negative. The teams are given an issue, called a proposition. They debate the proposition, taking turns presenting their arguments. The affirmative side goes first. They agree with the proposition. The negative side has to disagree. You're supposed to give evidence for your statements — it's not an emotional argument but a logical one. After both sides have made their opening statements, there's a break to allow each side to come up with a rebuttal. (Some of the boys in my class crack up when they hear that term, because it includes the word "butt." Give me a break.)

Anyway, during the pause, each team figures out how to respond to the other team's argument. That's what a rebuttal is — a response. Once both teams have presented their rebuttals (usually they are shorter than the opening arguments) and their closing arguments, the debate is over.

Except for the judging.

I forgot to mention that a judge (or a panel of judges) is listening to the debate. And at the end, the judge decides which team made a better case. That team is the winner.

I think debating is a blast, no matter which side you're on. It's fun to try to figure out how to convince other people to believe something. I liked it right away, as soon as Mrs. Simon introduced the unit. So I was excited when she told me she'd given Abby's and my names to Mr. Fiske, my English teacher from last semester. He's the one who found out about the convention in Washington, D.C. It's for middle school debate teams, and even though SMS doesn't have an official team, Mrs. Simon and Mr. Fiske thought it would be fun for a group of students to form a team now. They're going to come on the trip with us as our advisors. That's cool, because I really like them both.

They rounded up ten of us eighth-graders — I don't know any of the others well, except for Abby — and we practiced a little after school. And now we were headed to the Washington Challenge to try our skills against eighth-graders from all over the country. We'd be there for four days. Some of the time we'd be debating, but social events had been planned too, and there would even be time for sightseeing. I could hardly wait.

But first, back to that April night in my room. "So, what are you wearing for the first debate?" Abby asked, poking through the pile of clothes I'd stacked on the bed, next to my open suitcase.

"Same thing I always wear," I said, surprised. I'm not exactly a trendsetter. In fact, Stacey says I'm "fashion challenged." "Jeans and a T-shirt. Why?"

"I think we're supposed to dress up a little," Abby said. "Didn't you hear Mrs. Simon say that?"

"Ugh," I answered. "I probably blocked it out. Do I have to wear a skirt?" I cringed at the thought. A skirt means pantyhose, and pantyhose means a slip, and nice shoes, and — oh, it's all just too uncomfortable even to think about.

Abby grinned. "I think you'd be okay wearing cords or nice khakis," she said. She jumped up to rummage through my closet. "How about these?" she asked, pulling out a pair of neatly pressed khakis I've worn maybe twice. She didn't even listen for my answer. She just folded them carefully and added them to the pile by my suitcase. Then she turned back to the closet, muttering something about blouses.

Abby's like that. She takes charge.

Sometimes it bugs me. But I think I know why: It's because I'm the same way. Abby and I have had some "moments," I guess you could say. We don't always agree on how things should be done, but both of us are always positive that we're right. When she was in the BSC, this was a problem. In the club, I've always been the one to come up with new ideas and figure out how to make them real. The other members weren't likely to challenge me, but then Abby breezed in and, right away, started second-guessing me and even putting in her own ideas and opinions.

Mary Anne says it's good for me to be questioned that way. It doesn't *feel* all that good. But she's probably right. Don't get me wrong, I like Abby. We're friends. It's just that she's not always so easy to be friends with.

Abby is very competitive, and so am I. We love sports, but she's more of a natural athlete than I am. I enjoy coaching other players more than anything. Abby likes to be the star of the team.

It's amazing that she's so good at sports, considering that she struggles with both asthma and allergies. Abby has determination, that's for sure. And determination and talent are a great combination when it comes to sports.

"What about shoes?" Abby's question snapped me back to the present.

"Shoes?" I repeated blankly.

"You're not wearing those stinky old running shoes, are you? Those won't work at all with the khakis. How about some loafers or desert boots?" Once again, she rummaged through my closet. I had to smile.

When she'd arrived that night, Abby had announced that she was there to help me pack. So this was her way of helping: She was taking over. "Abby," I said, "I have packed for trips before, you know."

"I know. It's always good to have another opinion, though."

I wondered how she would feel if I went to her house and started criticizing everything she'd packed. Not that I was about to. Instead, I just sighed and gave up. I sat down in my inflatable easy chair and let her finish my packing.

"This is going to be such a cool trip," said Abby. "You and I will actually be able to hang out, the way we never have time to do here. I'm always busy with team practices and stuff, and you have your family and the BSC and *your* team practices. Now, for four days, we'll have time to just relax and enjoy each other's company."

Abby had a point. It would be relaxing to be away from all my responsibilities. My life can be overwhelming at times. My family is huge: I have two older brothers, Charlie and Sam, plus one younger one, David Michael. The four of us, plus our mom, are very close, partly because we struggled together in the years after my dad walked out on our family. Now my mom has a new husband. (Watson's a millionaire. We live in his mansion.) And I have three new younger siblings: Andrew and Karen, who are Watson's kids from his first marriage, and Emily Michelle, whom Watson and my mom adopted from Vietnam soon after they married. Emily is two and a half.

As if my family didn't keep me busy enough, I also run the BSC and coach a softball team for little kids. (The team is called Kristy's Krushers. Cute, no?)

I enjoy being busy, but I knew I was also going to enjoy some time away. Some good debates, a little sightseeing — it was going to be an awesome trip. Abby had been smart to grab the affirmative side on *that* debate. There was no way I could argue the negative.

Chapter 2

"We're here, because we're here, because we're here, because we're heeeere . . ."

"I can't take it anymore," Abby moaned, holding her hands over her ears. "Make them stop, someone, I beg of you! Before I go stark, raving mad!"

I cracked up.

So did Melissa.

It was Thursday, and the three of us were sitting on a bus that was headed for Washington. It was filled with kids from several Connecticut schools. Our SMS team had joined with some others to charter a bus. Melissa Banks sat across the aisle from Abby and me. I know Melissa a bit, though I haven't hung out with her much. She once went on a field trip to Philadelphia with Claudia and Abby, who all have the same social studies teacher. I think she drove

Claudia kind of nuts, but Abby seemed to like her well enough. I was keeping an open mind. She'd been assigned to room with Abby and me, and I was hoping we'd get along.

"Okay, guys, that's about enough of that one," Mr. Fiske called to the boys in the back of the bus. "How about trying a different tune for awhile?"

"Thank you, thank you," Abby gushed to Mr. Fiske. "I was about to lose my mind completely."

"We can't have that, can we?" said Mr. Fiske. "We need all the brainpower we can get for the next few days."

The boys in the back started up again. "We will, we will ROCK YOU!" they chanted, stamping their feet to the beat.

Mr. Fiske held up his hands. "This isn't a basketball game," he called. "Let's keep it down, okay?"

The boys kept on singing, in whispers, "We will, we will rock you!"

Abby and I looked at each other and rolled our eyes.

"Losers," said Melissa from across the aisle. "Right?"

I shrugged. "They're just obnoxious, that's all." I didn't know any of them terribly well, although Rick

Chow and Trevor Sandbourne have been in a couple of classes with me.

Melissa nodded. "*So* obnoxious," she agreed. "But they're boys, what do you expect?"

"Not all boys are obnoxious," Abby commented.

"No, of course not," Melissa said quickly. "Just — a lot of them are. Sort of. At least sometimes."

Abby and I exchanged a quick glance. I had the feeling we were both thinking the same thing. Was Melissa really cut out for debating? She seemed awfully wishy-washy. Eager to please.

"So, do you like debating?" I asked Melissa.

"Sure. It's okay, I guess."

"I love it," I said.

"Me too," Melissa admitted. "I just didn't want you guys to think I was a geek or something because I like to debate."

"Why would we think that?" Abby asked. "If you were a geek for liking it, we would be too. We're all going to the same convention, right?"

Abby's logic was excellent. In fact, what she had just said was a perfect example of what Mrs. Simon had called "deductive reasoning." That's taking a known truth — all cats have whiskers, for example

— and showing how it applies to a specific instance: Tommy is a cat, therefore Tommy has whiskers.

Or, if all people who like debating are geeks, and Kristy and Abby like debating, then Kristy and Abby must be geeks.

Only problem? We're not. The logic doesn't hold up. Because not all people who like debating are geeks. I could have destroyed Melissa's statement in five seconds' worth of rebuttal time. But Abby had already taken care of that.

"Right," Melissa answered, looking embarrassed. "Of course. I didn't mean — "

Abby lifted a hand. "Don't worry about it," she said.

Melissa smiled gratefully.

"So, want to play Travel Scrabble?" she asked, pulling the game out of her backpack.

I checked my watch. It was only eight-thirty, and we'd been on the bus for an hour. Mrs. Simon had said the trip would take about six hours. We had a long way to go. I leaned back into my comfy seat and sighed. "Sure," I answered. "Why not?"

The three of us played one full game — Abby won by about a gazillion points — and started another, but partway through it I began to feel sleepy.

The boys had stopped making noise and the bus was quiet. I looked down at my letters. Q, A, X, I, I, I, O. I didn't see any excellent words coming out of that mess. "Know what?" I asked. "I think I'm ready for a nap."

Melissa and Abby decided they were tired too. We'd woken up early to catch our bus. I settled down in my seat, pulled my jacket over my face, and drifted off into a dream about debating Bart Simpson, who kept telling me not to "have a cow, man" every time I tried to make a point.

I was pretty sure I was going to win the debate, but I'll never know, because I woke up before the judges made their decision. It wasn't a pleasant awakening either. "Hey," I said, picking up a jelly bean that had fallen into my lap. The boys in the back were rowdy again, and they were tossing jelly beans all over the bus.

"Hey," echoed Abby, waking up just as suddenly. Bleary-eyed, she looked at the piece of candy that had hit her. "Looks like green apple flavor," she said musingly. "My favorite." She popped it into her mouth. Then she made a face. "Ack!" she cried, clutching her throat. "I've been poisoned!"

"What?" I panicked. "Should I call Mr. Fiske?"

Abby laughed. "No, no, nothing that bad. It's just the wrong flavor. Jalapeño instead of green apple."

Melissa, who'd woken up by that time, had to put in her two cents. "Yuck," she said. "I hate jalapeño too."

"I don't exactly *hate* jalapeño," Abby said. "I was just expecting green apple, that's all."

"Oh," Melissa said. She picked a jelly bean off her sleeve. "Look, I have grape." She held it up. "Anybody want it?"

When Abby and I shook our heads, Melissa ate it. Then she yawned. "I'm so bored. Do you guys want to play Scrabble again?"

"Maybe later," I said.

"I know," suggested Abby. "Let's play car-color bingo. Anna and I play it whenever we're on a long car trip. It's simple — you just pick a color, and the first person to spot a car that color gets to yell 'Bingo!' Then that person picks the next color."

"Cool," said Melissa. "What color should we start with?"

"Let's make it hard," said Abby. "How about — hmm — turquoise?"

We all stared out the windows for awhile. I saw

tons of white cars, red cars, green cars, and black cars. I even saw a purple car. The person driving it, a woman with bright red hair, looked up at me and smiled and waved as she passed the bus. I waved back. "Let's see how many drivers we can get to wave back to us," I suggested. "While we're waiting for a turquoise car, I mean."

We started keeping track. About one out of every three drivers waved back. Women drivers were more likely to wave back, and of course if kids were in the car they waved like crazy. Some people smiled when they waved, some people did silly waves, some people looked deadly serious.

The three of us were cracking up. Then, all of a sudden, Melissa yelled, "Bingo! Bingo! Bingo!" She was yelling and pointing out the window on her side of the bus. Abby and I stood partway up so we could see the car she'd spotted. Sure enough, this huge old turquoise car was motoring alongside the bus. It was a convertible with lots of chrome and huge fins sticking up in back where the taillights were. It was the kind of car Watson loves, the kind he calls a "classic."

"Nice one," Abby told Melissa. The three of us waved at the driver, a young girl with short black hair and cool-looking black-framed yellow sunglasses. She grinned and waved back. Then she honked the horn and waved some more.

"Girls," said Mrs. Simon, coming back to see what we were up to. "I'm not sure this is the safest thing to be doing. The other drivers need to concentrate on the road, you know." Then she glanced out of Melissa's window. "Ooh, an Impala!" she cried. "Cool car. I had a boyfriend in high school who had one of those."

See why I like Mrs. Simon so much? She's not like other teachers.

We promised to calm down, and Mrs. Simon went off to check on the boys in back, who were singing again by then. "Comet, it makes your teeth turn green," they sang. "Comet, it tastes like gasoline!"

"Check it out!" said Abby, pointing to a sign we were passing. "We're almost there."

We settled down and gazed out the windows as the bus worked its way into the city. Into Washington, D.C.! I was pretty excited. Soon we were in the middle of the city, passing official-looking buildings. People on the street looked sophisticated and busy. They walked fast, some of them talking on cell phones as they strode along.

"Look, there's the President!" yelled one of the boys in the back. We all stared out the windows.

"Where? Where?" I asked.

"Made you look," said the boy. I glared at him.

"Hey," Abby said. "Pennsylvania Avenue. We're crossing the street the President lives on."

"Sure, sure," I said. I wasn't about to be fooled again. But I snuck a glance anyway. Abby was right. We had just crossed Pennsylvania Avenue. The White House couldn't be far away.

Soon after that, the bus pulled into the semicircular driveway of a big hotel. "Here we are!" said Mr. Fiske from up front. "Let's head on in to register and find our rooms. And please, stay together. It's going to be a madhouse in there, with kids arriving from other schools."

He was right. The lobby of the hotel was packed with eighth-graders. The hotel had set up several temporary registration tables, each one labeled with a big sign. EASTERN STATES, read the one Mr. Fiske led us to. I spotted signs for SOUTHWEST STATES, MIDWESTERN STATES, and ALASKA. Kids were here from everywhere! It was a little overwhelming, especially since the noise level in the lobby was majorly high.

Then the weirdest thing happened.

I spotted someone I knew! It was a boy who used to go to SMS. What was his name? I frowned, trying to remember. Then it came to me.

His name was Terry. Terry Hoyt.

I'd always wondered what happened to him.

❀ Chapter 3

"Lucas!" Melissa yelled. She took off running across the lobby, toward Terry. Or, rather, toward the boy standing next to Terry.

"Lucas," she cried again, wrapping her arms around the boy. He was tall, with hair so blond it was almost white. He had a pale complexion too, although at that moment he was blushing so fiercely his face was brick-red.

Melissa finished squeezing the breath out of him and turned back to Abby and me. "Come here, you guys!" she called. "Meet Lucas."

Abby and I joined them, and Melissa made the introductions. "These are my friends Abby Stevenson and Kristy Thomas," she said. "This is Lucas Goodman." The way she said his name made me want to roll my eyes. She was gazing at him the way a puppy gazes at its owner. Was she going to start wagging her tail?

"Nice to meet you, Lucas," Abby said.

Lucas nodded and smiled at her. He was still blushing, but I noticed that when he looked at Melissa, his face showed the same puppy-dog look she wore.

"Hi," I said. "So, where are you from?"

"Lucas is from right here in Washington," Melissa explained before he could open his mouth. "His father is a congressman. He and I met at camp last summer. Camp Minawaskee. In Maine." She closed her eyes and sighed, and I had the feeling she was reliving some romantic memory.

Ugh.

"So you're from Washington, but you're staying at the hotel?" I asked, confused.

Lucas nodded. "It's part of the convention experience," he explained. "It wouldn't be the same if we didn't stay here. Have you ever been to one of these conventions before? They're awesome."

Abby and I shook our heads. Melissa just kept gazing at him. I had the feeling she hadn't heard a word he'd said.

"I went to one last year," Lucas continued, "but

this is David's first time. Oh — sorry. This is my friend David. David Hawthorne. We're roomies here." He looked to his left, where Terry Hoyt had been standing. "David?" he called, when he realized nobody was there.

Then I saw Terry Hoyt again. He'd moved away, toward another group of kids. I happened to catch his eye and I smiled. For a second I thought he recognized me — but then he looked away.

"David!" Lucas called again.

I saw Terry glance around. Then, reluctantly, he approached us.

"David, this is Kristy and Abby and — Melissa." The way Lucas said Melissa's name made it clear how he felt about her. So did the sappy smile he gave her as he made the introductions.

"David?" I asked. "But — "

"David Hawthorne," he said, sticking out a hand.

I shook it, even though I was confused.

"I could have sworn you were somebody else," I told him. "Didn't you go to Stoneybrook Middle School? In Connecticut?"

Did he react to the name of the school? I couldn't tell. He looked at me, then looked away. He shrugged. "Nope," he said into the air. "Never heard of the place. You must have the wrong guy."

"You look *exactly* like this boy I used to know a little," I told him. He did too. Terry had the same brown hair, the same hazel eyes. In fact, I remembered Stacey, who had known Terry best (I think she had a little crush on him), going on and on about how special his eyes were, "all filled with gold flecks." Terry had been pretty cute, in fact. So was David. I saw a few of the girls in the crowd checking him out.

David shrugged again. "Maybe we were separated at birth," he cracked. "Who knows?"

I decided to let the subject drop. "Well, it's nice to meet you anyway," I said. "Have you been debating for a long time?"

He shook his head. "Nope."

"Oh." This David Hawthorne person didn't seem to believe in long explanations. "Me neither." The conversation sort of stalled there.

Just then, I heard someone calling my name. I turned to see Mrs. Simon waving to me from across the room. "Kristy," she called, "Abby, Melissa, over here! I thought we talked about staying together." She looked irritated.

Every kid in that crowded lobby was staring at us

by then. I put my face down to try to hide the fact that I was blushing. "Let's go, you guys," I muttered to Abby and Melissa.

"See you," Abby said to Lucas and David.

Melissa's good-byes took a little longer. She and Lucas had this long hug. Then they stared into each other's eyes a little longer. Then they hugged again, whispering into each other's ears. You'd have thought they were saying good-bye for a year or two, instead of for a couple of hours. "I'll see you at din-din, Mookie," Melissa promised. She walked off, waving, moving backward, so she could see Lucas for as long as possible.

In my opinion, there's nothing more icky than being around people in that early, gooey stage of love.

"Who's the boy, Melissa?" asked Mrs. Simon when she'd rejoined the group.

"Oh . . . nobody," Melissa said, looking dreamy. "Just a boy I met at camp."

Mrs. Simon arched an eyebrow. "And you just happened to run into him here? What an amazing coincidence."

"Isn't it?" Melissa didn't seem to realize that Mrs. Simon was being sarcastic.

I saw one corner of Mrs. Simon's mouth turn up

as if she were hiding a smile. "Well, anyway, girls. Here's your room key. We're all on the fifth floor. I'm just two doors down from you, so try to keep things down to a dull roar."

Abby took the key. "Five-nineteen," she said. "Cool."

"You can find your way up and unpack," Mrs. Simon told us. "The welcoming dinner starts at five-thirty. That should give you plenty of time to freshen up and change your clothes."

Melissa was already drifting off. Abby and I looked at each other, grinned, and followed her toward the elevator.

"Well," Abby whispered, before we caught up with Melissa, "that explains a lot. Lucas, I mean. No wonder she wanted to come down here."

I nodded. "And what about his friend? I'm telling you, there's something weird going on there. You never met Terry, but I swear, this guy looks *exactly* like him."

"He acts a little suspicious too, if you ask me. Like he has something to hide."

"What?" said Melissa. By then we'd caught up to her near the elevator.

Abby and I exchanged a glance. "Nothing," I said.

Melissa seemed to accept that. She was still looking all gooey. "So?" she asked. "What did you think? Isn't he totally awesome?" She hugged herself.

"He's beyond awesome," Abby said with a straight face.

"I know." Melissa sighed.

The elevator dinged, the door opened, and we climbed aboard. A minute or two later, Abby was unlocking the door to room 519. "Excellent!" she said as the door swung open. "Check it out!"

We walked in and looked around. It was a big room with two double beds and one twin-sized bed, all covered in pink-and-purple flowered quilts. In one corner was a seating area, with comfy-looking armchairs and a small table. Along one wall was a bureau with a big TV sitting on top of it. A picture window ran along another wall, and through the open curtains I could see a balcony.

Melissa went into the bathroom. "Cool!" we heard her cry. "There's a whole bunch of tiny little shampoos and conditioners. Enough for everybody."

Abby headed for the balcony, opened the glass door, and stepped outside. "I think that's the Kennedy Center," she said, shading her eyes as she looked off into the distance. "Mr. Fiske said it was near here."

"I'll take the twin bed," I volunteered, sitting on it and bouncing a little to test how firm the mattress was.

We unpacked, stacking our casual clothes in the bureau drawers and hanging up blouses and skirts and dress pants in the closet. We staked out areas on the bathroom counter for our toothbrushes and things. Melissa had brought a whole bunch of makeup, plus a blow-dryer. Her stuff took up twice as much room as Abby's and mine put together.

Melissa kept chattering about Lucas. She told us how she'd met him. Then she moved on to their first date and first kiss. And then she filled in the details of the e-mails and phone calls they'd shared since the summer. "He's so sweet." She sighed again. "Didn't you think he was sweet?"

"The sweetest," I agreed.

"Couldn't be sweeter," said Abby.

"And adorable," Melissa cooed, pausing to hold the sweater she was folding up to her cheek.

"Very adorable," Abby said.

"The adorable-est," I put in.

Melissa didn't notice the amused glances Abby and I were sending each other. She was head over heels in love and wouldn't have noticed if thirteen elephants had come crashing into our room. She probably would have asked them if they thought Lucas had the cutest nose in the universe.

We dressed for dinner. For me, that meant putting on my newer pair of cords. For Melissa that meant putting on a blue blouse — Lucas's favorite color, of course. Then we headed downstairs. The dining room was already filled with kids. Some of them were seated at big round tables, while others milled around looking for friends from past conventions.

Melissa spotted Lucas the instant we walked in. She headed straight for him. David Hawthorne was sitting at his table, so I followed Melissa, and Abby followed me.

"Where did he go?" I asked when we'd worked our way through the crowd. David had disappeared.

Abby shrugged. "Looks like he found another place to sit." She nodded toward a table on the other side of the room. David had just pulled out the last empty chair and was taking his seat.

He glanced at me as he sat down, then looked quickly away. I had the feeling that he was avoiding me. But why?

✳ Chapter 4

The dinner was fun, but it went on a little too long. At least five people made speeches welcoming us to the convention, and by the fifth one I was starting to feel drowsy. In fact, I think I nodded off a couple of times. I don't know why sitting on a bus all day makes you so tired, but it does.

By the time we returned to our room, I was ready for bed. It was an effort to find and put on my pajamas, but I managed. Then I passed out and slept like a rock until our wake-up call came at eight the next morning. Like a rock, that is, that gets woken up a few times by another rock sneaking in and out of the room to meet her boyfriend.

"I guess she and Mr. Awesome had plans," Abby said to me, rubbing her eyes as she sat up in bed. Melissa was in the bathroom, blow-drying her hair.

"I guess so," I agreed. "I just hope she doesn't get us in trouble."

"Good morning," Melissa said cheerfully when she emerged from the bathroom. She was fully made up and her hair was perfect. She didn't look nearly as tired as I would have expected, considering that she'd had a few hours less sleep than Abby and I had had. "Isn't it exciting? Today's the first real day of the convention."

"Very exciting," Abby replied, climbing out of bed. She stretched and yawned. "I guess we'll find out about our teams this morning."

Abby and I had signed up for the Mixed Debate Competition, General Level (that's for beginners like us). We would be assigned to three-person teams, each member of which would be from a different school. Melissa wasn't going to be on a team. She had signed up for an event called Extemporaneous Speaking, which I didn't know much about, except that it sounded hard. A bunch of the other kids on the SMS team were doing Extemporaneous Speaking too, and some of them were doing one-on-one debates.

Abby and I dressed, and the three of us headed downstairs to breakfast. Melissa and Lucas found each other immediately. It was as if a special force field drew them together. We took four seats at a table near the front of the room. David Hawthorne was nowhere in sight.

"Good morning!" A dark-haired man in a very snazzy gray suit was standing on the stage. He was one of the people who had spoken the night before. He had an English accent and very good diction. (That's when you pronounce all your words carefully and correctly. It's a good quality in a debater.) I couldn't remember his name.

"I'm Arthur Greenleaf, for those of you who have forgotten," he continued, as if he'd read my mind. "And as the director of this year's convention, I'm pleased to start things off by announcing our topics." He paused to look over his glasses at a piece of paper he held. "First, the advanced debaters. You will be discussing the following proposition. Resolved: That U.S. immigration policies contradict American ideals."

A murmur ran through the dining room. Abby and I exchanged glances. I could tell she was thinking the same thing I was: No way were we ready for advanced debating.

"I look forward to hearing our debaters on that topic," said Arthur Greenleaf. He looked down at his paper again. "Intermediate debaters will be presented with another fascinating proposition. Resolved: That journalists have a right to protect confidential sources of information."

Yikes. That sounded pretty hard too. I wouldn't know where to begin with a topic like that. I guess you have to do lots and lots of research. But how would those teams have time? The more experienced debaters must be used to it, I figured. Nobody was bolting for the exits, anyway.

"And now, for the general debaters," said Arthur Greenleaf, smiling, "we have a topic that has been debated almost since the beginning of human life."

I drew in a breath, crossed my fingers, and looked at Abby. What was it going to be? If it had anything to do with politics or history, I was going to be in deep trouble.

"Resolved," continued Arthur Greenleaf, "that cats make better pets than dogs."

Everyone burst out laughing.

What a relief. I would have no problem with that topic. Of course, everyone knows dogs make better pets. I mean, cats are okay, but come on: Dogs rule. My old dog Louie was the best pet ever, and the puppy my family has now is pretty awesome too. So, as long as I was on the negative team, I'd be able to sail through the contest. And, for some reason, I'm always assigned to the negative team.

"Now," said Arthur Greenleaf, "my able assistant will help me assign teams for the Mixed Debates."

A woman walked onto the stage, carrying a red-white-and-blue top hat.

"Inside this hat are slips of paper with your names and schools on them," said Arthur Greenleaf. "Red slips are advanced debaters, white slips are intermediate, and blue are general. We'll pick three names for each team. Please stand when you hear your name read, so your team members can spot you. After breakfast, you are free to meet with your team in order to plan for the first round of debates, which will take place this afternoon."

The woman held up the hat, and Arthur Greenleaf began picking out names for the teams. Behind them, another man wrote down the names on a large chalkboard.

The noise level in the room grew as the names for the advanced teams were read out. A lot of kids had been coming to conventions like this one for a couple of years now, and they all seemed to know each other. Cheers would go up when some names were read. The teachers in the room kept trying to quiet their kids down, but it was no use. Instead, Arthur Greenleaf just kept reading in a louder and louder voice.

Things settled down a bit as he read out the names for the intermediate teams. I guess those kids didn't know each other as well. And by the time Mr. Greenleaf began reading the names for the general teams, hardly anybody was even paying attention. Some of the advanced and intermediate kids were already up and moving around.

There were six general teams. Abby was named to the first one, along with a boy from South Dakota and a girl from Tennessee. I'd sort of forgotten that she and I wouldn't be on the same team.

Arthur Greenleaf read off a bunch of other names before he pulled mine out of the hat. I was the first member assigned to Team Six. When he read the name of the second member, it sounded like Kite-A-Dow, but when the man behind him wrote it on the blackboard, I saw that it was Kai Teh Tao. Arthur Greenleaf said he was from New Jersey.

Finally, the last member of our team was announced. "David Hawthorne, from right here in Washington, D.C." David! I looked around to see if I could spot him, since I hadn't seen him yet that morning. He was way in back, and he stood up only for a second. I had to hide a smile. He wasn't going to have much luck avoiding me from now on.

Next Arthur Greenleaf announced which teams would argue the positive sides of their propositions and which would argue the negative. Guess what? For the first time in my debating career, I was assigned to the positive. I couldn't believe it. I was going to have to argue that cats make better pets than dogs.

Abby's team was assigned to the negative. Lucky her. She looked at me, smiling, and faked a big sneeze. Abby is majorly allergic to dogs — but not, as strange as it seems, to cats. I had to laugh.

When all the teams had been assigned and the sides determined, we were dismissed for the next few hours. Debates wouldn't begin until four that afternoon, so we had plenty of time to prepare. As soon as Arthur Greenleaf turned us loose, everybody started milling around in the dining room, trying to find their team partners.

"Hi," I heard someone say behind me. "Aren't you Kristy?" I turned to see Kai Teh Tao. "I'm Kai," he said, smiling shyly.

"Have you seen David Hawthorne?" I asked, craning my neck to look around at the crowd.

"He's in back," Kai said, pointing. "Should we go find him? We might as well meet for a little while right now."

"Sure." I had a feeling it was going to be awkward being on David's team. He seemed so nervous around me. I decided it might be best to make it easy on him. So as soon as Kai and I found him, I spoke up. "Hi, David," I said.

He smiled a thin smile.

"Listen," I continued. "I was thinking this morning. I figured out that I must have mixed you up with somebody else. Now that I think about it, the boy at our school was a little taller than you. Anyway, I never knew him that well. He was really better friends with a friend of mine, Stacey McGill."

I thought I saw his eyes light up when I said Stacey's name. Really, I did. But I let it go. "So, anyway, here we are on the same team. That's cool, isn't it?"

He nodded. "Except for one thing," he said.

"What's that?" I asked.

"I can't stand cats," he answered, grinning for real now.

Kai and I burst out laughing. "I don't mind them," I said, "but no way are they better than dogs."

Kai agreed. "Give me a big, slobbery Labrador retriever any day," he said. "Cats are so stuck-up."

"Oh, well," I said, throwing my hands in the air. "I guess we're going to have to consider this a challenge. I bet if we really work at it, we can even convince *ourselves* that cats are better."

Kai nodded and held up his hand for a high five. "We can do it," he said.

David put up his hand too. "Let's get to work."

We found a quiet corner of the lobby and sat down to brainstorm. David took notes as we blurted out every positive thing we could think of about cats. Some of them were pretty silly. For instance, Kai said they are less likely to bark at the letter carrier. But a lot of them were serious. "Cats need less care," I pointed out.

"And they eat less," added David.

"But think how stinky their canned food is," I said, holding my nose. "Yuck."

"Forget about that," said David. "Dogs eat canned food too. Besides, we have to concentrate on the good stuff."

"I know, I know," I answered. We worked for an hour or so, putting together a very solid opening argument. Then we decided it was time for a break.

"Let's go to the Mall," suggested David.

"Shopping?" I asked. "I hate shopping."

David shook his head. "No, the Mall in D.C. isn't about shopping at all. It's the area where all the monuments are. The Capitol building is at one end, and the Washington Monument is at the other. It's a cool place to walk around."

"Sounds great," I said. I was glad to see that David was acting more comfortable around me. We headed out of the hotel — and bumped into Melissa on our way. She wanted to come with us, but first she had to find Lucas (of course). She ran inside and returned with not only Lucas but Abby.

"Hey, cat lovers," Abby crowed when she saw us. "You guys are dead meat. Can you think of even one good thing to say about cats?"

I laughed. "Don't get me started. Did you know that cats were worshipped in ancient Egypt? And what about their habits? Cats are so much cleaner than dogs. Plus, they can practically take care of themselves, and — "

Kai nudged me. "Don't give away all our arguments," he whispered.

Abby grinned. "It doesn't matter," she said. "Dogs are so much cooler it's not even a contest. I mean, can you play fetch with a cat? Or teach it to shake hands?"

"Some cats can — " I began, but David interrupted me, hustling us all out the door.

Abby and I debated all afternoon as David and Lucas showed us around the Mall. But it was all in fun.

At least, I thought it was.

Chapter 5

"And so, based on their persuasive arguments, their excellent reasoning, their speaking skills, and the quality of their rebuttals, I award this debate to the affirmative team, Team DKK." The judge smiled down at us.

Yesss! I had to fight the urge to do a victory dance and throw my fist in the air. That kind of behavior apparently isn't considered appropriate at a debate. Instead, it seems, you stand there smiling at your teammates. Then you shake hands with the other team (no chants of "two, four, six, eight" either) and thank the judge.

If you haven't already guessed, Team DKK is *my* team: David, Kristy, and Kai.

Kai and David looked as happy as I felt as we walked out of the room. "We did it!" David said.

"Your rebuttal was excellent," I told him as we gave each other a high five. "The other team thought they had us with that hairball argument, but you came right back at them."

Kai laughed. "I think our opening arguments were awesome too. We had all the strongest points lined right up. And you spoke really well, Kristy."

We had planned to take turns doing opening arguments, and I'd been a little nervous about being the first on our team to do one. But it had gone well. I'd tried to remember everything I'd learned about speaking clearly and concisely, and I'd remembered to use natural-looking gestures to emphasize certain points.

Suddenly, I was exhausted. And starving. "Isn't it time for dinner?" I asked.

Kai checked his watch. "The dining room should be open," he answered. "Want to go see?"

"You guys go ahead," said David. "I'm, um, going to go change first." Suddenly, he seemed uncomfortable again. I had the feeling he didn't want to sit at a table with us, where the conversation might be less about cats and dogs and more about personal things.

That was fine. Kai and I sat with Melissa, Abby, and Lucas, and we had a good time. We chatted with this great brother-sister debating team, Alexandra and Scott Toombs, who were in the two-person event. After dinner a dance was held in a big meeting room on the third floor. The lights were low, and the DJ was playing dorky music from the eighties. Abby and Kai and I hung out near the refreshments table, but Melissa and Lucas headed for the dance floor. They danced every dance as if it were a slow one, no matter what the beat. They looked as if they were in a different world.

After awhile, Abby glanced at me. "Want to get out of here?" she asked. "We can go hang out in our room."

"I'm so ready," I answered. "You don't mind, do you, Kai?"

He shook his head. "I'm out of here too," he said. "See you tomorrow, okay? We should do some more preparing before our next debate. Come up with some fresh arguments."

"Definitely," I said. "Team DKK has to stay on top."

"You're not the only ones who won today," Abby pointed out. "Don't start getting cocky." Her team (they'd named themselves Team Lincoln, after Abraham Lincoln, one of the best debaters in history) had won its first round too.

When we arrived back in our room Abby closed herself in the bathroom to relax in the tub, and I headed for the phone. I'd been thinking, ever since I met David Hawthorne, that I'd like to check with Stacey about her memories of Terry Hoyt. I plopped down on the bed and dialed Stacey's number.

"Stacey, it's Kristy," I said when she answered.

"Kristy!" she said, surprised. "Is something wrong?"

"Not exactly."

"Aren't you in Washington?"

"Yup. But there's something I wanted to ask you about. Some*one*, really. It's Terry Hoyt. Remember him?"

Stacey hesitated. "Uh, sure," she said after a couple of seconds. "I remember Terry. Why?"

"It's just that there's this guy at the debate convention who looks exactly like him," I told her. "But he swears his name is David Hawthorne, and that he's never heard of Stoneybrook. Weird, huh?"

"Very weird." Stacey sounded strange. "David Hawthorne, you said?"

"Right. He lives here in D.C., and he's on a debate team. He's here with his friend, who happens to be Melissa's boyfriend. This guy she met at camp. They're all over each other. It's really gross."

Stacey was silent.

"Stace?"

"Oh, right. Gross. I heard you."

"Anyway, I just wanted to know if you had any idea what happened to Terry. He moved away pretty suddenly, didn't he?"

"Uh-huh. I don't know where to, though."

"So you lost touch with him?"

"Right. We lost touch."

I thanked Stacey, said good-bye, and hung up, feeling as if she wasn't telling me something. But if she didn't know, she didn't know. Terry was probably in California or Oklahoma or somewhere, clueless about the fact that he had a double who was living in Washington.

I didn't have much time to think about our conversation because the phone rang as soon as I hung up. "Hello?" I said.

"Kristy, it's Kai. I was just thinking — as long as we're not at the dance, maybe Team DKK should spend some time tonight practicing for tomorrow."

"Great," I said. "That will really give us an edge."

"I'll call David," said Kai. "We can meet in the lobby, okay?"

"See you in ten minutes," I said.

"Where are you headed?" asked Abby, who had just emerged from the tub. "What's going to give you an edge?"

"I'm meeting with David and Kai."

She raised her eyebrows. "You guys are serious."

"I guess we are." I put my notebook and a couple of pens into my backpack and headed for the door. As I left, I noticed that Abby was already on the phone, calling *her* teammates.

I stepped into the hall and saw someone walking toward me from the other end.

It was David.

"Hey," I said.

"Oh! Hey," he answered. He didn't look entirely thrilled to see me.

"Kai called," I said. "Did he call you too?"

David nodded. He looked over his shoulder, toward his room.

"So, what do you think we can do differently tomorrow?" I asked, ignoring his weird behavior.

"Um," said David, glancing over his shoulder again as we walked toward the elevator.

"I think we should be more aggressive with our arguments," I suggested. "You know, really jump in. If we leave any room for doubt, the other team will pick up on it."

David nodded. "Uh-huh." I had the feeling he wasn't really listening.

"So, have you come up with any more good reasons why cats make better pets?" I asked.

David drew a little closer to me and muttered something under his breath.

"What?" I figured he was being secretive, in case someone from another team was listening, which seemed overly cautious to me. After all, we were walking down an empty hall.

"I said, we're being followed," David repeated, just loudly enough so I could hear him.

"Followed?" I grinned. "You mean, by somebody from a rival team?"

He shook his head. And he didn't smile back. Instead, he glanced over his shoulder yet again. As he did, we came to a corner. On the wall ahead of us was a large mirror, mounted over a table holding a vase of flowers. I looked into the mirror. Sure enough, someone was walking far behind us, a man in a dark shirt and black jeans.

"How do you know he's following us?" I asked, keeping my voice low in order to humor David.

"He's not following us," David answered in a whisper. "He's following *me*. So go on."

"What do you mean?" I asked indignantly. If

David really was being followed by some strange guy in dark clothing, I wasn't about to take off and leave him alone to deal with it. "I'm staying with you."

David frowned. Just then, we reached the elevator. I stretched a finger toward the DOWN button.

But David grabbed my hand. "Come on," he said, pulling me toward the stairway door, which was directly across the hall from the elevator. "Run!" He opened the door and shoved me through it. Then he yanked the door shut behind us and we scrambled down the stairs. Above us, the door opened and shut again as the man entered the stairwell.

David really was being followed.

I ran, my heart beating hard with excitement — and fear.

We ran down three flights of stairs, then one more, and then we started down another. The man drew closer every second. I felt as if I were in a chase scene in some action movie. It was almost as if this were happening to someone else.

"We're nearly at the lobby," David said, panting. "Keep running, Kristy."

We were just a few steps away from the bottom of the stairs — the door to the lobby was in sight — when the man lunged for David. I screamed as loudly as I could, while David shoved the man away.

The man staggered backward, nearly fell, then caught himself. "Not so fast, Hawthorne," he said. "Your father is going to pay." He lunged a second time and grabbed David by the shirt.

I screamed again.

"Run!" David yelled.

I flew down the last steps, threw open the door to the lobby, and ran screaming toward the desk. Within moments, four security guards appeared. "A boy is being kidnapped!" I yelled, pointing toward the door to the stairs.

They sprinted for the door, and I followed them. When they opened it, neither David nor the man was in sight.

But David's backpack lay on the landing, papers spilling out of it.

Two of the guards ran down the stairs toward the basement and the indoor parking garage. The other two ran up.

I had a feeling that I should follow the ones who had headed downstairs, so I did. As soon as we burst through the door into the parking garage, I spotted David. The man in the dark clothes was dragging him toward a long black car. "There he is!" I yelled, pointing. The guards sprinted toward the man, who pushed David to the ground and took off, running.

"David!" I cried. "Are you okay?" I helped him up as the security guards chased after the kidnapper. A young woman who had been behind the reception desk appeared next to me.

"I'll help you," she said, taking David's other arm. We supported him as he rose shakily to his feet.

"Are you okay?" I repeated.

David thought for a moment. "I guess so," he said, sounding dazed. "Just a little bruised." He took a few limping steps. "I don't think anything's broken."

We helped him hobble to the stairway. As we made our way toward the lobby, the security guards reappeared — empty-handed.

"You didn't catch him?" I asked.

They shook their heads.

The kidnapper was out there somewhere.

Chapter 6

The security guards escorted David, the receptionist, and me back into the hotel lobby. One of them spoke into his radio, reporting what had happened. He must have been talking to the police because two officers — a man and a woman — arrived just seconds after we stepped through the stairwell door.

"Is there somewhere we can talk?" one of the officers asked the receptionist.

She looked pale. "Oh — sure," she said. "Let me just check with the manager. You can probably use his office." She ran off, leaving David and me with the police and the security guards. I was still feeling shaky, and I could only imagine how David must have been feeling. It was very reassuring to be surrounded by four people in uniform, four people who would protect us and keep us safe.

The woman officer, who introduced herself as Sergeant Driscoll, checked with David to make sure he wasn't hurt. Meanwhile, the other officer, Officer Michaels, took statements from the security guards about what they'd seen and heard.

Then the receptionist returned and led David, the officers, and me into a small, quiet office behind the reception desk. "You can use this room for as long as you like," she told the police. She still looked pale. Before she left, Officer Michaels took a short statement from her.

Sergeant Driscoll sat David and me on the small couch that took up one wall of the office. Then, after a closer look at David's bruises, she decided one of them could use some ice and went off to find the hotel manager. That left us with Officer Michaels, until his radio spluttered and a voice began talking. He excused himself and stepped into the hall to answer it.

"Kristy," David whispered as soon as we were alone, "there's something I have to ask you."

"What?" I asked, leaning closer to him. He looked tense, frightened.

"I don't know if you remember what that guy

said to me about my father having to pay. You haven't mentioned it yet, so maybe you forgot. Anyway, keep it to yourself for now. Okay?"

I frowned. "But shouldn't we tell the police? That could be a big clue."

David glanced nervously toward the door. "Look," he said. "The thing is — the thing is, my dad will want to be involved in this. And he may not want the police to know — " He stopped and sighed. He looked at the floor, as if he didn't want to meet my eyes.

"What?" I asked. "David, what are you saying?"

He started talking low and fast. He still wasn't looking at me. His gaze wandered from the floor to the walls. "What I'm saying is that you were right when you thought my name was Terry Hoyt. That *was* my name, for just a little while. My family lived in Stoneybrook because my dad was on a case there. He's a Secret Service agent, and at the time he was working undercover. Now he has a regular posting, here in D.C. Our family is trying to live normally for a change."

I gasped. I was having a hard time taking all of this in. "Wait — you mean — " I began.

"I'll explain more later," said David. "But for the

time being, the police don't have to know everything. My dad is a regular agent now, but it's important that his past identities remain secret. It could be dangerous for him — and for me — if the wrong people had certain information." Suddenly, he looked hard into my eyes. "Do you understand?"

I nodded, then shook my head. I was so confused. "Not really," I said. "But I'll do what you say."

A look of relief came over David's face — just for a second. Then the tense look returned. "Good. Thank you, Kristy. Thanks for trusting me."

Sergeant Driscoll arrived with the ice then, and Officer Michaels walked in behind her. They hovered around David for a few moments. I watched, thinking. Was I crazy to trust David? His story was so wild, so unlikely. Maybe I was putting myself in danger by believing him. Maybe *he* was the bad guy.

Then I remembered how friendly Stacey had been with Terry Hoyt. If he were some kind of criminal, she would have figured it out. Wouldn't she? Or if he were telling the truth, maybe Stacey already knew that "Terry" was David. Maybe she knew and hadn't told any of us. I thought about my conversation with her and remembered her reaction when I asked about Terry. It sounded as if she'd been hiding something.

As I sat thinking, there was a knock at the door. Sergeant Driscoll opened it, and I saw Mrs. Simon. "I understand one of the students from my school is here," she said. I felt like running into her arms, but instead, I just smiled at her.

"Mrs. Simon!" I said.

"Kristy, are you all right?" She hurried toward me.

"I'm fine," I told her.

"Not hurt?" she asked, putting her hands on my shoulders and looking into my eyes.

I shook my head, suddenly feeling as if I could start crying at any minute.

"I was chaperoning the dance when I heard," Mrs. Simon said. "I came as quickly as I could."

"Thank you."

There was another knock at the door, and a man I hadn't seen before entered. "Dad!" David exclaimed. He jumped up to hug the man, who I now noticed looked a lot like David.

I checked out Mr. Hawthorne carefully as he introduced himself to me, Mrs. Simon, and the police. Could he really be a Secret Service agent? He looked like your basic, everyday dad. Then again, if you're going to work undercover, average looks are probably helpful.

"Now that you're both here," said Sergeant Driscoll to Mr. Hawthorne and Mrs. Simon, "we'd like to question these two about what happened."

"Is that okay, Kristy?" Mrs. Simon turned to me. "Do you feel up to it?"

"Sure," I said.

"I do too," David said before his dad could ask. "But there's not much to tell. It all happened so fast."

We went over our stories, from the moment David had realized he was being followed until the time the receptionist and I helped him up off the ground in the parking garage. We described the man in the dark clothes and told about the chase down the stairs. Neither of us said anything about the kidnapper's mentioning David's father.

The police asked a lot of questions, and Mr. Hawthorne added a few as well. We went over our story at least three times, from different angles. Finally, Sergeant Driscoll said we were nearly done.

The officers read over their notes one last time. Officer Michaels turned to me. "Are you sure you've told us everything?" he asked. "There was nothing else, nothing the man in the dark clothes said or did?"

I hesitated — just for a millisecond — and shook my head. "That's it," I said. "I've told you everything I remember." In a way, I wasn't lying. Until David had reminded me, I'd forgotten that the kidnapper had mentioned David's father. The chase scene was a blur in my mind, because it had happened so quickly.

Officer Michaels looked at me. "You're *sure*?" he asked.

I nodded.

Just then, his radio came to life again. "We're needed elsewhere," he said after he'd listened carefully. "So that's it for now. But we may be checking in with you later. Meanwhile, I'm leaving you two under the care of your guardians." He nodded at David. "Take care of that bruise."

Then he and Sergeant Driscoll said their good-byes and left. Mrs. Simon stood up. "I'm afraid I should head back to the dance," she said apologetically.

"That's fine," said Mr. Hawthorne. "I'll stay with Kristy and David until we've figured out how to keep them safe and sound."

"Is that okay with you?" Mrs. Simon asked me.

"Sure," I said. "I'll be fine."

Reluctantly, she let me go. "All right," she said. "I'll check on you later. And I'll let Kai know what's going on."

When she left, the room was quiet for a few seconds. Then Mr. Hawthorne turned to David. "Does she know?" he asked, nodding toward me.

"I had to tell her," David admitted.

"All right, then," said Mr. Hawthorne. "So, what weren't you telling the police?" He sat down at the desk where Officer Michaels had been sitting and pulled a little notebook out of his pocket. He didn't waste any time getting down to business.

David told him what the kidnapper had said.

"I thought it might be something like this," his dad mused. "It may be that this man is someone I helped to apprehend, who has some resentment toward me."

"That's what it sounded like," said David.

"So, here's what we'll do," Mr. Hawthorne continued. "You'll come home with me, and I'll make sure that a security team keeps an eye on Kristy. Just until we've caught the man." He snapped his notebook shut.

"No, Dad," David said quietly.

"What do you mean, 'no'?"

"I'm not going."

I looked from face to face. Mr. Hawthorne seemed surprised. David looked stubborn.

"I want to stay at the convention," David went on. "I've been preparing for this for a long time. I want to be here with my friends. You said that part of the reason you gave up undercover work was so we could have a normal life, didn't you?"

Mr. Hawthorne nodded slowly. "True. But this man could be dangerous."

"So why couldn't the security team watch Kristy *and* me?" David asked. "I mean, if we let the bad guys decide what we can and can't do, then it's as if they're running our lives, isn't it?" He looked earnestly at his dad. "Remember, you've taught me how to take care of myself. They'll catch this guy any minute, and the whole thing will blow over. I don't think it's fair to make me miss the convention because of this."

Mr. Hawthorne smiled and held up his hands. "All right, all right," he said. "I can see you've been practicing your debating. You make some very good points." He smiled. "And I have some good friends who are going to be watching you two very, very carefully."

And that's how I ended up with my own Secret Service agent.

✳ Chapter 7

They followed us through the lobby and toward the elevator. I tried not to look at them, but I couldn't help sneaking glances. Did other people notice them? To me, they seemed to stick out like penguins at a polar bear party.

Our Secret Service agents. Two clean-cut men in dark suits, white shirts, and shiny black shoes. Both with tiny wires snaking from inside their suits up to their ears.

At least they weren't wearing sunglasses.

Mine was Agent Melendez. David's was Agent Sanford. They'd introduced themselves, then told us that from that moment on we were to ignore them and let them do their job. They were there to protect us, plain and simple.

But how easy is it to ignore guys who look like

that? All the other people in the hotel — even the ones who *weren't* eighth-graders — were dressed in tourist clothes or regular workday clothes. Melendez and Sanford did not exactly blend in.

But what did I know? These guys were pros. Who was I to question their outfits?

Mr. Hawthorne had stayed with us in the manager's office until Agents Sanford and Melendez arrived. He'd been reluctant to turn us over to them, but he'd made a deal with David and he was going to stand by it. He seemed like a nice dad. He gave David a hug before he let us walk out of the room with our agents. "Be careful," he warned us. "And have fun at the convention."

"We will," David promised. "Hey, did I tell you that our team won our first debate?"

Mr. Hawthorne looked impressed. "Good work," he told us. "Okay, go on and get some rest."

Now we were on the elevator, along with our agents and a couple of other people. I noticed a woman staring at Agent Melendez's ear wire, and then, following his steady gaze, at me. I had a feeling she thought I was somebody important, the President's niece or someone. I almost expected her to ask for my autograph. But then there was a ding-ing sound and the elevator door opened at the fifth floor. David and I walked off, trailed by our new shadows.

I stopped at the door to my room. "Want to come in for a minute?" I asked David. According to the rules Mrs. Simon and Mr. Fiske had set, boys were allowed in our room as long as it was before "lights out" time, which was at ten. It was only nine, so we wouldn't be breaking any rules.

David looked unsure.

"Come on," I said. "I'll even buy you a soda from the minibar." A minibar is a little fridge in a hotel room. It's stocked with soda and candy and stuff, and you're charged for the things you eat and drink. Watson had warned me not to raid the minibar too often, since most hotels charge very high prices for whatever you take. So far, Melissa and Abby and I had been able to resist. But tonight felt like a bit of a special occasion. It's not every day you're chased by a kidnapper.

"Okay," David said. He followed me into the room. I held the door open for a second and looked back at Sanford and Melendez, a question in my eyes. Melendez shook his head slightly as he took up a post against the wall opposite my door. I nodded. I understood that they would stay right there, keeping watch. In fact, I had a feeling they'd do it all night.

Nobody else was in the room. I figured that Abby must be out practicing with her debate group, and Melissa was probably still dancing the night away in Lucas's arms.

David took a seat in one of the armchairs, but he didn't relax into it. He sat there looking uncomfortable as I rummaged around in the fridge. "How about a Coke?" I asked. "Or root beer?"

"Coke is fine."

I handed him a cold can. "So," I began, taking a seat in the other armchair. "Interesting evening, wasn't it?"

David gave me a tiny smile. "Kind of."

I could see he wasn't going to talk about it without some prodding on my part. "Your father seems really nice," I said. "You're lucky."

"He's a good guy." David looked down at his Coke. I had the feeling he was used to keeping things inside.

I wasn't.

"You know what? I was really, really scared," I confessed, suddenly unable to hide it for one second longer. "That guy — he was dangerous." I'd been trying to stay calm, not wanting the grown-ups to overreact and make us leave the convention. But it hadn't been easy. Now that we were alone, I could open up.

David nodded slowly. He looked up at the ceiling and let out a long breath. "I know," he said. "I was scared too. Terrified, actually." Then he met my eyes. "I don't even want to think about where that guy would have taken me, or what would have happened next. You might have saved my life, you know."

I shook my head. "I didn't do anything. All I did was scream and run."

"That was enough," said David. "Anyway, thanks."

"You're welcome." I held up my root beer can. "Let's have a toast to escaping the kidnapper."

We clinked cans. David seemed to relax a bit as he took another sip of his soda.

"You must have had a pretty exciting life," I said carefully. I was dying to hear more about what it was like being the son of a Secret Service agent.

David shrugged. "Not really. It isn't as if things like that happen every day."

"No, but it isn't as if your dad's a shoe salesman either. I mean, you've probably lived in all kinds of interesting places. And you've had all these different identities too. Have you had other names besides Terry Hoyt?"

David nodded wearily. "About ten," he said. "You get really tired of it, though. It's not always easy to remember what your name is, and what your dad does, and where you live, and where you lived before, and all the other things you're supposed to know each time around."

I nodded sympathetically. "So what were some of your other names?" I asked. I couldn't help myself.

"Well, when we lived in Seattle for awhile I was Justin Peterson. That was when I was about nine. Dad was working on a case involving smugglers."

"Wow."

"I liked Seattle," David admitted. "I had a good friend there. Steve, I think his name was. I can't even remember anymore. The people I've met are all mixed up in my mind."

"I bet you remember Stacey, though," I said.

He nodded, smiling ruefully. "Of course. Stacey McGill. She's very cool. I liked her a whole lot."

"Does Stacey — does she know what your dad does? Did you tell her?"

He nodded again. "But don't be mad at her for not telling you. I made her promise."

"I understand."

"Will you tell her I said hi?" he asked.

"Absolutely." I settled back in my chair, and he did too. For a second I felt guilty about being so comfortable, when Agents Sanford and Melendez were standing out in the hall. I mentioned it to David.

He laughed. "Oh, don't worry about them," he said. "That's their job. They're used to it."

"Have you ever had agents follow you around before?" I asked.

"This is the first time. And the last, I hope."

"I have to admit, I don't mind it so much. I mean, what if that guy did come back to try again? Now he knows that I know what he looks like. He might come after me too." I shuddered.

"Don't worry," David said. "Those guys out there will make sure you're safe. They're professionals."

"So, who do you think that man is?" I asked. "The kidnapper, I mean."

"I don't know. My dad has helped put away a lot of criminals. There could be any number of people walking around with grudges against him."

I whistled and shook my head. "What a life."

"It's been interesting," said David. "But I definitely prefer the way things are now. Dad's not un-dercover anymore, and we can use our real names. I'm allowed to tell people what he *really* does for a living. Things are a lot easier when you can just be yourself!" He smiled at me, looking happier than he'd seemed in hours. "And it's good to be settled in one place. I mean, I'm glad I've seen some other places, but this city is cool. I've made some good friends here, and I like our house. I want to stay put for a good, long time."

Suddenly, I heard the door open behind me. I have to admit I jumped.

"Hey, we heard all about what happened!" Melissa said, bursting into the room with Lucas in tow.

Abby was right behind them. "What's with Heckle and Jeckle out there?" she asked. "They're not too friendly, are they?" She was glancing behind her, into the corridor. I couldn't see Sanford or Melendez, but I could imagine their expressionless faces.

I giggled. They'd be Heckle and Jeckle in my mind from then on.

"Is it true you almost got kidnapped?" Melissa asked David. "I heard the guy had a gun. I heard he grabbed you!"

"Whoa, whoa." David held up his hands. "I didn't see any gun."

"But he did grab you, didn't he?" asked Melissa. "Why? What was he after?" She was like a dog with a bone.

David shrugged, looking tired all of a sudden. "I don't know," he said. "My dad's a Secret Service agent. That could have something to do with it. But nobody knows for sure."

"Everybody's talking about it," Abby added. "Word travels fast around here."

"I'm sure there are all kinds of rumors," David said. "But I doubt many of them are true."

"So are those guys out there, like, guarding you?" Lucas asked, nodding toward the door.

"Just for a little while," David answered.

"Cool, dude."

"Right." David met my eyes. I knew exactly what he was thinking.

His new, "normal" life wasn't so normal after all.

❋ Chapter 8

"DKK rules!"

"Yesss!"

"All right, team!"

Kai, David, and I did a three-way high five. It was Saturday morning. We had just emerged from Debate Room One, where we'd won another round in the tournament.

"We really do make a good team," I said to them. "Somehow we complement one another."

"Sure. You have the big mouth, Kai has all the brains, and I supply the charm and charisma. How can we miss?" David joked.

Kai and I cracked up. The three of us were getting to know one another pretty well. And the experience David and I had gone through had brought us closer. Only people I know and trust can call me a bigmouth and get away with it.

We had one more debate that afternoon, and if we won we'd head to the finals. It was hard to believe. After all, I hadn't been debating for very long. But I guess with my big mouth, I'm a natural.

"I think your buddies enjoyed the show too," Kai said, with a nod to Agents Sanford and Melendez, who were standing about ten feet away in a doorway.

David rolled his eyes. "They're starting to bug me," he said.

I really couldn't complain. They made me feel safe. And boy, was I going to have a good story to tell when our trip was over. Having a Secret Service agent of your own did take some getting used to, though. Agent Melendez had been waiting in the hall when I stumbled out of my room first thing that morning on my way to breakfast. Had he been there all night, watching my door? Or had another agent covered the night shift? Melendez and Sanford had stood by while David and I chowed down on pancakes and eggs. After breakfast, Melendez had followed me back upstairs, while Sanford shadowed David. I took a quick shower, dressed in my "good" clothes for the debate, and stepped into the hall to find faithful old Melendez still waiting. He didn't even have a newspaper with him or anything. I couldn't help wondering if he was bored. I certainly wasn't providing him with any entertainment.

He may have enjoyed the debate, though. I know I did. In fact, I was so involved in it that I forgot he and Sanford were there. The team we had faced was good, and their arguments for dog superiority had been inventive and funny. Still, we managed to shift our rebuttal to one that destroyed their whole strategy. And even though David might have been joking about his charm and charisma, he really did have a certain presence. He could run for office someday, he's that good at public speaking. Throughout the debate, he seemed relaxed and confident. The shaky David I'd seen the night before had disappeared. If he thought about the kidnapper at all, you wouldn't have known it. He acted like a person without a care in the world. And he still seemed relaxed now, even though he was frowning a little in Sanford's direction.

Abby and her team emerged from Debate Room Two. She was grinning, and she let out an exuberant

"Yahoo!" when she saw me. Her teammates looked pretty happy too.

She ran to me, waving to Melendez as she passed him. "Excellent debate," she reported.

"Ours was too," I said.

"I heard the team you were debating against wasn't so great," Abby replied. "I bet you beat them easily."

Well. Did she think we weren't good enough to beat a strong team? "As a matter of fact, they were very good," I told her. "But we were better."

She shook her head, smiling. "Beats me how you can come up with even one argument in favor of cats."

"Well, you'll hear more than one if our team meets yours in the finals," David put in.

Thank you, David.

Abby just smiled again. "So," she said, turning to me, "want to go sightseeing?"

I looked at David and Kai. "I don't know. I think we might want to practice a little more, right, guys?"

"For sure," said Kai.

"I'm there," said David.

"Guess I'll see you later," I told Abby. She looked bummed. "Want to go to Melissa's event with me later this morning? I'm dying to see how she does."

"Sure." Abby looked happier. "I'll see you there."

David and Kai and I (and Agents Sanford and Melendez) headed for the coffee shop for a snack before we got down to work. Then the five of us went upstairs to David's room. Sanford and Melendez settled themselves in the hall while we made ourselves comfortable on the couch and chairs inside.

We discussed the debate we'd just won, breaking it down until we had covered every angle. Facing a good team is helpful. You hear new arguments, which gives you the chance to come up with counter-arguments. For our next debate, we would start out with those ideas.

"And we'll ditch the argument about cats shedding less, since apparently, it isn't true," Kai said as we finished up an hour or so later. He made a note on his pad. "Then we'll add the one about lower overall costs."

"Sounds good," I said.

Just then, there was a knock at the door. David opened it.

An annoyed-looking Mr. Hawthorne poked his head in. "Shouldn't you check to see who it is?" he asked.

"Why, when our buddies are out there?" David asked. He looked a little annoyed himself.

"You have a point," Mr. Hawthorne admitted. "But still, safety first." He introduced himself to Kai, then asked if he and David and I could have a few minutes alone together. Kai said he had some stuff to do in his room anyway. He took off after we'd agreed on a time to meet before our afternoon debate.

Mr. Hawthorne set his shiny black briefcase on the coffee table and opened it up. "I brought some pictures for you two to look at," he said. "I'm hoping you can help identify our friend from yesterday."

He handed over a stack of photos. David started flipping through them. "Nope, nope, nope," he muttered as we looked at each face quickly.

"Wait a minute," I said, stopping him. "What about that guy?"

David studied the photo I was pointing at and shook his head. "No," he said. "Our man had a bigger nose and darker hair."

He was right. I realized that, as the son of a Secret Service agent, David was probably a lot more observant than I was.

He flipped through a few more photos. "I don't think the guy's in here," he said as he reached the bottom of the stack. "Oh, wait a minute." He slid out one photo and took a closer look. "What do you think?" he asked me.

I examined the picture. The man had a beard and mustache, while our kidnapper had been clean shaven. But there was a familiar look to him. "Maybe," I said.

David showed the photo to his dad. "Do you have another shot of this guy?" he asked.

Mr. Hawthorne rummaged in his briefcase. "What about this?" he asked, handing us a smaller picture. David and I leaned over it together. This time, the beard was gone.

"That's him!" David said. "Right?"

I nodded. "I think so." I looked again. "Yes, I'm almost positive. That's the guy."

Mr. Hawthorne took the photo from David. Looking at it, he shook his head. "Dibdin," he said.

"Excuse me?" said David.

"His name is Lance Dibdin," Mr. Hawthorne explained. "He was part of a group of computer hackers we busted up a few years ago. We caught him in a sting operation. I think he did some time, but maybe he's out now." He thought for a second. "No, that's not right," he continued. "He never did go to prison. He was freed on a technicality."

"Is he dangerous?" I asked.

Mr. Hawthorne looked at me. "He could be. He certainly has no fondness for me. But the police are already looking for him, and they should be able to track him down quickly." He checked the picture again. Then he smiled at us. "Meanwhile, I think you'll be safe. But quit opening your door without checking to see who's there." He tousled David's hair. "I mean that."

"Okay," said David. "Just let me know as soon as Dibdin is picked up. I don't want those guys hanging around any longer than they have to." He nodded toward the door. Sanford and Melendez were probably out there listening. Or maybe those ear wires they wore were connected to a bug in David's room. I wouldn't be surprised.

After Mr. Hawthorne left, David and I headed down to Debate Room Three to catch Melissa in action. Abby was already there, sitting in the front row with Lucas. Lucas was also doing extemporaneous speaking, but he had won his round earlier in the day. Abby waved to us. "I saved you some seats," she called.

The extemporaneous speaking contest was totally different from team debating. There were three judges sitting at a table in front of the stage. One by one, the contestants came out. The judges would throw a statement at them and tell them to defend it, and the contestants would have to speak about that topic for ten minutes — with no preparation! Loud mouth or not, I myself couldn't do it.

Some of the kids weren't so hot. They stumbled around and said "um" a lot. One boy even looked as if he might start to cry at any minute. On the other hand, Rick Chow from SMS was pretty good. But guess who ended up winning the round?

Melissa.

She was awesome! When it was her turn, the judges told her to defend the proposition "The chicken came first." (As in, "Which came first, the chicken or the egg?")

Melissa started talking and she didn't stop until the timer went off. She was funny and persuasive and intelligent sounding. I hate to say it, but she was like a different person up there. Abby and I kept exchanging surprised looks as she spoke. I don't think either of us believed our ears.

Afterward, when the judges had awarded her first place, she joined us at our seats.

"You were excellent," said Lucas, giving her a kiss.

Melissa giggled. "Really?" she asked, looking

into his eyes. "Wow, thanks. Did you really think I was good?" She giggled some more, and — I swear — batted her eyelashes at him.

Abby and I exchanged one more glance and a little smile. Melissa was still Melissa.

✻ Chapter 9

Want some good news? Team DKK won its Saturday afternoon debate. That meant we were on our way to the finals!

Want some bad news? Abby's team won too. That meant they were on *their* way to the finals. We'd be up against each other. Which in itself wasn't such a bad thing. Other than Melissa, we were the only SMS students still in the tournament — Trevor Sandbourne and his partner had lost in the two-on-two debate to Alexandra and Scott Toombs. So it was pretty cool. It was just that Abby and I could hardly talk to each other anymore as it was. Every conversation turned into a debate. Now the situation would be even more intense.

Some more bad news? The police hadn't been able to find Dibdin yet. David checked in with his dad after our debate, and all Mr. Hawthorne could say was that they were still looking. Bummer. That meant Agents Sanford and Melendez would be with us for awhile longer.

I could deal with that, but I could tell David was just about fed up. He couldn't stand being followed around. I'd seen him shooting dark looks at Agent Sanford during our debate. But there was nothing we could do. David had made a deal with his dad, and if having a shadow was the only way he could stay at the convention, he was going to have to have a shadow.

Speaking of shadows, I was beginning to get tired of the Melissa-and-Lucas show. Those two were practically joined at the hip. Everywhere he went, she went. Everywhere she went, he went. They finished each other's sentences, gazed into each other's eyes, and seemed clueless about how nauseating their behavior was.

"Guess what!" Melissa shrieked when we ran into each other in the hall that afternoon. I was with David, Kai, and Abby. She was, of course, with Lucas. "I'm in the finals!" The standings for extemporaneous speaking had apparently just been posted in the main lobby.

"Congratulations," I said. "That's excellent."

"I know. And guess who the other finalist is?" She was holding Lucas's hand, and now she swung it back and forth, smiling coyly (oh, ew) at him. "My Lukie, that's who!"

Lucas blushed. (At least he had the sense to be embarrassed.)

"Wow," David said. "Dueling sweeties. *That* should be interesting."

My eyes met Abby's. We may not have been able to agree on much lately, but we agreed on one thing: This was bad news. Melissa versus Lucas? She was sure to dissolve into giggles and baby talk in front of the judges.

"Anyway, we're going to celebrate by doing some sightseeing," Melissa told us. "Want to come? We thought we'd check out the Smithsonian. They have an entire museum devoted to television and movies."

"Sounds cool," Kai said. "I'll go."

David shrugged. "I've been there a million times. I think I might just chill for awhile."

Abby and I decided to go. "I want to change first, though," I said. I was still in my debate clothes.

"So do I," Abby agreed. "How about if we all meet in the lobby in fifteen minutes?"

She and I headed for our room. Melissa lingered

for a moment, saying good-bye to Lucas before she followed us. (How could they stand to be parted for so long? Fifteen minutes! What a tragedy.)

Abby and I were silent until we hit the elevator. Then, once we were alone (except for Agent Melendez, of course), she burst out with it. "What are we going to do about Melissa?" she cried.

"We're going to have to talk to her. If she blows the finals, she'll regret it later."

"I wouldn't know what to say," Abby confessed.

"I would. I'll do it." I had no problem telling Melissa exactly what I thought.

Which is what I tried to do as soon as she walked into the room a few minutes after we'd arrived. She started sorting through the T-shirts she'd brought, looking for something to change into.

"Melissa," I began, "can I talk to you for a second?"

"Sure," she said, holding up a purple shirt and checking herself in the mirror. I had the feeling she was wondering if Lucas liked purple.

I jumped right in. "I know Lucas is very important to you. And I know it's going to be hard to go up against him in the finals."

"You're right."

"I am?"

"Yes. It *will* be hard. Lucas is really smart. You guys haven't seen him in action, but he's an excellent speaker." Now she was holding up a pink shirt. "He liked this one when we were at camp," she murmured to herself.

"I'm sure he's good," I agreed. "Otherwise he wouldn't have made the finals. But that's not what I meant."

"So what did you mean?" she asked, throwing down the pink shirt and picking up a yellow top.

"Well, just that I wouldn't want to see you — " I paused. "How can I say this? I just don't want you to back off. You shouldn't give up winning the finals just because you and Lucas are, you know — " This wasn't as easy as I'd thought it would be.

"What Kristy's trying to say is," Abby jumped in, "you shouldn't let Lucas win just because you like him."

"Well, duh!" said Melissa, staring at us. "Are you guys out of your minds? I would never do that. No matter what Lucas means to me, this is the finals! I plan to kick butt. I just hope Lucas doesn't mind too much when I walk away with that trophy." She turned to head for the bathroom, throwing the yellow shirt over her shoulder. "But thanks for the advice anyway!" she called.

Abby and I looked at each other, stunned.

And yet, when Melissa and Lucas reunited in the lobby, it was as if they hadn't seen each other in six months.

I almost lost my lunch.

As soon as Kai arrived we set off for the Mall. The Smithsonian Institution is actually made up of a whole bunch of museums and libraries — and even a zoo! There was more to it than we could see in a day, or a week, for that matter. We decided to start at the museum with the TV and film stuff, just because it sounded like fun. I glanced back at Agent Melendez once in a while as we walked, hoping he would find this outing a little more interesting than his duty had been so far. I couldn't tell if he was enjoying himself. He wore the same straight-faced expression, no matter what. I was beginning to wonder if he ever smiled.

I thought of David, back in his room. I was glad, personally, to know that Agent Sanford would be sitting outside that room, guarding David. After all, whether David liked it or not, there was a good reason those agents were following us.

As we walked along, Kai and I talked about that day's debate. Abby tried to jump into the conversation once in awhile, but everything she said sounded as if it belonged in Debate Room One. She baited me with comments about the uselessness of cats, and I bit, coming back at her with my own observations about the relative brainpower of dogs. We argued back and forth until Kai jumped in, his hands in the time-out position. This happened three times. Finally Abby gave up and left Kai and me on our own to talk and plan strategy for the next day's debate.

But I forgot about debating when we arrived at the museum. There was so much to see!

"Check it out," cried Kai as we rounded a corner. "A phaser from the original *Star Trek* series. I'd give anything to own that."

"I like this statute of Charlie Chaplin," Abby said. "He's one of my heroes." She posed next to it and asked Melissa to take her picture (even though I was right there).

Melissa and I agreed on our favorite item: the ruby slippers worn by Judy Garland in *The Wizard of Oz*. We stood in front of that display case for a long time, talking about our memories of watching that movie.

"I wanted to be Glinda, the good witch, when I grew up," she confessed. Lucas smiled at her. I think he was picturing her in a beautiful ball gown, carrying a wand.

"Not me," I said. "I wanted to be the Scarecrow. I wanted to be able to dance the way he could."

"What was the scariest part for you?" asked Melissa. "Mine was the flying monkeys."

I shuddered. "Oh, definitely. They were majorly scary. But what about those trees with faces? I had a bad dream about them when I was six. I never forgot it."

"Can I just point out one thing?" Abby asked. "Please note that one of the stars of this movie is Toto. A dog, not a cat." She gave me a smug look.

I rolled my eyes. "Oh, please," I said. "What does that have to do with anything?"

"I'm just pointing it out," she repeated. "I'm just saying that a dog makes a more interesting character in a movie than a cat would."

"Oh, yeah? Well, tell me this. What about the Cowardly Lion? He's a cat, isn't he?"

A security guard approached us, a finger to her lips. "Keep it down, girls," she warned us.

Oops. Abby and I exchanged angry looks and moved on.

The rest of the afternoon was like that. Abby and I couldn't agree on a thing, and we brought up the cat-dog issue constantly. Finally, Kai and Melissa and Lucas separated us. They told us we had to stay ten steps away from each other or go back to the hotel.

When we did return to the hotel a couple of hours later, we were in for a surprise. An agent I hadn't seen before approached us as we walked into the lobby. (How did I know he was an agent? Take a guess. The ear wire is a pretty good tip-off.) "Do you know where David Hawthorne is?" he asked without even introducing himself.

We shook our heads. "Isn't he here?" I asked.

"He hasn't been seen for two hours," said the agent. He looked grim. "He's missing."

❁ Chapter 10

"Missing? What do you mean, missing? How can he be missing?" Suddenly, my heart was racing. "He has to be here."

The man shook his head. "He's not in the hotel," he said.

"Well, he probably went for a walk or something. I'm sure he and Agent Sanford are just out sightseeing."

The man stared down at me, still wearing that grim look. He was tall and lanky, with salt-and-pepper hair. "Agent Sanford has been taken off duty," he told me. "I'm his replacement. Agent Westcott."

"Off duty? Well, that explains it, then. He left, and David went out for a walk. No big deal." I couldn't even think about the other possibility: that the man in dark clothing had returned. Lance Dibdin. The man who wanted to kidnap David.

"You don't understand," said Agent Westcott. "Agent Sanford was taken off duty *after* David Hawthorne disappeared."

Abby, Kai, Melissa, and Lucas had been listening to this exchange, swiveling their heads back and forth as if they were watching a tennis match. Now Abby gasped. "You mean David disappeared while that guy was supposed to be watching him?"

Agent Westcott gave a tiny nod.

"Whoa." Lucas raised his eyebrows. "I'll bet *he's* going to get detention."

"Agents don't get detention, silly," Melissa said.

"I know, I was just kidding. But the dude must be in serious trouble."

"Forget about Sanford. What about David?" I was practically shouting.

"We'll find him," Kai said firmly.

"The police have been notified," said Agent Westcott. "And of course the Secret Service is involved. We'll take care of it."

I shook my head. "We want to help. Where should we look first?"

"Please, leave this in the hands of professionals." Agent Westcott sounded final.

"Forget it, Kristy," Kai said, grabbing my arm. "Let's just go up to our rooms and wait. There's nothing else we can do."

Agent Westcott looked approvingly at Kai. "Good idea, young man," he said.

I thought Kai was nuts. But he tugged on my arm and pulled me away.

Melendez paused to talk to Westcott. I realized he must already have known that David was missing. He'd probably heard about it over his ear wire. As soon as we were out of earshot, Kai said in a loud whisper, "We'll organize our own search. I bet we'll find him first."

Melissa, Lucas, and Abby were ready. So was I. "Where should we start?" I asked.

"I'm thinking," said Kai. "We had a conversation yesterday about his favorite places in the city. I know he mentioned the Lincoln Memorial. I'm trying to re-member others."

"We should check his room," Melissa said. "Lucas and I can start there and then go over the rest of the hotel. There may be places the agents missed."

"Good," said Kai. "Go right now. We'll figure out some other places to look. Just meet back in the lobby in" — he checked his watch — "forty-five minutes. Okay?"

Melissa gave him a little salute. "Yes, sir," she said, smiling.

"I think we should help check the hotel again," said Abby. "Maybe they missed him."

"How about if we all fan out and do that?" asked Kai. "Then, if we don't find him, we can figure out where to look next."

"Good," Abby said.

They both looked at me. I was still a little in shock, I think. I kept picturing Dibdin's face. The others didn't know how scary he'd been. But I did. And it wasn't at all hard to imagine him grabbing David while Agent Sanford was looking elsewhere. That man had been determined. I wasn't so sure David was going to be easy to find.

"Kristy?" asked Abby. "Are you okay?"

"Sure," I said. I glanced behind me and saw Agent Melendez standing nearby. The sight of him made me feel better somehow. If Dibdin *was* around, I was happier than ever to know I had my own personal guard. "I'm fine," I said. "Just tell me where to go." Even though I'm usually the one who organizes things, this time I was glad to let Kai be the leader. I felt as if my brain were working overtime, trying to understand what had happened. How could David have just disappeared?

Suddenly, I realized that David had become a friend. I hadn't known him long at all — even if you count the time I knew him as Terry Hoyt — but I felt close to him. I cared about what happened to him.

"Why don't you look in the areas where the convention is taking place? And Abby can check the dining room and the coffee shop." Kai was taking charge.

"Okay," said Abby.

"And should we meet in the lobby?" I asked.

Kai nodded. "Right. Same plan as we made with Melissa and Lucas."

I glanced back at Agent Melendez again. If he knew what we were up to, he didn't show it. He looked ready to follow me wherever I went, as usual. "Okay," I said. "See you guys soon."

We went our separate ways. Melendez tailed me, as I headed for Debate Room One, my first stop. It was empty. Debates were over for the day. Debate Room Two was empty also. There were a few people in Debate Room Three. Judges, I think. But no David. I hadn't really expected to find him there. I wandered around the halls for awhile, then decided to head back to the lobby and check the spot where the debate standings had been posted. Melendez followed me. I was in no particular hurry, since I was early for the meeting we'd planned. I thought hard about where David might be. If Dibdin had kidnapped him, where would he have gone? David could be out of the city by now, or even out of the country.

As we entered the lobby, I was imagining David on a plane to Mexico, drugged and blindfolded. My imagination was running away with me, but I couldn't seem to control it.

The lobby was full of people coming and going. I spotted several Secret Service agents, including Agent Westcott, in the crowd. Then, in a deep armchair by the window, I spotted something else. A familiar-looking head of brown hair.

No. It couldn't be.

I walked closer and took another look. Sunglasses hid his eyes, but the boy sitting in that chair, calmly reading a newspaper, was definitely David Hawthorne.

"David!" I ran toward him. "You're safe!"

He looked up and took off the sunglasses. "No kidding," he said. "See? I don't need an agent to watch me."

I saw Melendez gesture toward Westcott. Suddenly, he and four other agents materialized in our corner.

"David Hawthorne?" Westcott asked.

"That's me," David said.

Westcott nodded and spoke into his sleeve for a moment. (There must have been a microphone in there). "Mind telling us where you've been?" he asked David.

David shrugged. "Out and about. I just went for a little stroll. Is that a crime?"

"How did you elude Agent Sanford?"

"It wasn't that hard," David replied. "I told him I was going to take a nap. I checked out in the hall after a few minutes, and he was away from his post for a second. So I took off."

"Why?" I asked. I was in shock all over again. I had been very relieved to see David, but now I felt another emotion taking over. Anger. I'd been so worried about him. How could he have done this to me?

"I was just sick of being shadowed, that's all," he explained. "I didn't go anywhere dangerous. I was around lots of people all the time. I'm not stupid."

"I'm beginning to wonder about that," a voice said. It was Mr. Hawthorne, who had just arrived. He must have heard about David's reappearance over the radio. His face was red, and he was frowning. "I thought you were intelligent. But this was a bone-headed move. You're coming home with me. Now."

"But Dad!" David protested. "The finals!" He looked at me for support. "Kristy needs me. My team needs me."

For a second, I felt like turning my back on him. What David had done was no joke. I was as furious as Mr. Hawthorne was. But I saw the plea in David's eyes and I couldn't ignore it. "We do need him," I said. "If he has to leave, our whole team will suffer."

Mr. Hawthorne nodded slowly. His face was a little less red already. "That's a good point, Kristy," he said. "There's no reason you should miss out on the finals just because David has behaved so irre-sponsibly."

I looked at David, and I could tell he was holding his breath. He probably had his fingers and toes crossed too. "I'm really sorry, Dad. I didn't think it would be such a big deal. I just needed to get away for five minutes."

"You're not the first person who has felt that way about being guarded," Mr. Hawthorne admit-ted. "But you did make a deal with me."

"I know." David looked ashamed. "I'm sorry."

"Okay, here's the new deal," Mr. Hawthorne said, just as Lucas, Melissa, Kai, and Abby showed up. "You can stay. But you have a new agent. Me. I'm off regular duty for the next twenty-four hours, but I'm reassigning myself. I'll be your guard. And I'm not going to take my eyes off you."

David let out a breath. "Thanks, Dad," he said quietly. "Thanks."

Mr. Hawthorne walked away with the other agents. They stood in a small group, talking and glancing at David.

Abby, Kai, Melissa, Lucas, and I clustered around David. "Where *were* you?" Abby asked.

"Just — out," said David. He looked at me and grinned. "Phew! That was close!"

I didn't smile back. "It's not funny, David. I thought Dibdin had grabbed you. I was really worried. Your disappearing act made a *lot* of people worry. And you got Agent Sanford in trouble."

He lost the grin. "I just — "

"I know you don't like being followed," I told him, "but you're just going to have to get over that. You almost jeopardized our chance to win the finals."

David hung his head. "You're right," he said. "You're totally right. And I owe you an apology. I'm

sorry, Kristy. Really I am. I apologize to all of you."
He looked at the others. "And I promise to behave
from now on."

What could we say? David was our friend. And
friends forgive friends when they mess up. I just
hoped he would keep his promise.

❀ Chapter 11

David stuck pretty close to our group for the rest of that evening. And Mr. Hawthorne stuck pretty close to David. I noticed that, as promised, he hardly took his eyes off his son. Throughout dinner, Mr. Hawthorne barely took a moment to glance at his plate as he worked through the steak and salad we were served. And afterward, when we went to a really cool dance performance at Kennedy Center, I noticed that Mr. Hawthorne spent a lot more time watching David and scanning the theater than he did watching the stage.

My friend Jessi Ramsey, who's a ballet dancer, would have loved this performance. It wasn't ballet, though. In fact, it was kind of the opposite of ballet. It was tap dancing, but not the kind Shirley Temple does in those old movies. This was *athletic* tap, danced by big, strong guys wearing black boots. It was awesome.

Afterward, we headed back to the hotel. I think we were all exhausted. It had been a long day, between the debates, the museum, and the search for David. When we arrived in the lobby, David said he was going to bed.

"Good," said Mr. Hawthorne firmly. "So am I. I've arranged to have a cot put in your room. It's okay with Lucas. You don't mind, do you?"

What could David say? He just gave his dad a weak smile. Then he turned to Kai and me. "Don't forget," he told us. "Team DKK rules!" He gave us a double thumbs-up. "See you tomorrow."

Lucas headed to his room too, with Melissa trailing behind. "I'm just going to say good night to Lucas," she called to us. "I'll see you in our room in a few minutes."

"Whatever," Abby said tiredly. She and I took the elevator to the fifth floor together. We didn't talk much during the ride, even though I tried once or twice to start a conversation. I guess neither of us wanted to argue, so it was easier just to stay quiet.

It was weird. I was looking forward to the next day's debate, but I wasn't feeling as confident as I had before. Not that I would have ever admitted it to anyone, especially to Abby. But here's the thing: In my heart, I just didn't agree with our position. Even after all this time, and even after all the work I'd done to convince other people that cats are better pets than dogs, I still didn't believe it. A lot of what Abby — and the teams we'd faced so far — said made sense to me. What can I say? I love dogs. Cats are okay, but that's all.

I was envious of Abby. She was lucky to be on the "dog" side. She must have felt much more confident than I did. Still, if my team had made it this far, maybe we had a chance of winning. I was going to have to work on my attitude. I would have hated for David or Kai to guess how I was feeling.

I was thinking this as we left the elevator and walked to our room, Agent Melendez trailing behind us. Oh, yes, he was still there. I was getting so used to him I hardly even noticed him anymore. But I had a feeling he'd enjoyed the tap performance nearly as much as I had. I had looked at him once and saw him *almost* smiling.

I was still thinking about the debate as I changed out of my clothes and into my pj's. I guess Abby was deep in thought too, because neither of us said much besides "The bathroom's all yours," or "Have you see my hairbrush?"

Eventually, both of us were stretched out on our beds. I was reading, and Abby was working on some notes for the next day's debate. There was a knock on the door.

Abby and I looked at each other. Who would be knocking at our door? It was after lights-out, so everybody was expected to be in their rooms. I wondered if it could possibly be Agent Melendez. Maybe he needed to use the bathroom or something. I jumped up and pulled a pair of jeans on over my pajamas. Abby did the same. Then I peeked through the peephole.

Guess who was there. Melissa.

"Oh, it's you," I said. "Why did you knock? Did you forget your key?"

Melissa giggled. "No, I have it. But I brought some company, so I thought I'd knock first and make sure you guys were decent." She stepped back a little so I could see who was standing behind her. Lucas.

"No way," I said. "It's after lights-out. Do you want to get us in trouble?"

"Oh, chill." Melissa made a face at me. "Nothing's going to happen. Let us in."

I checked with Abby. She shrugged. "I don't care, I guess. What's the big deal, really?"

"Oh, all right," I said. I unlocked the door, rolled

my eyes at Abby, and opened it. Melissa and Lucas squeezed past me into the room. Before I closed the door, I caught Agent Melendez's eye. I could have sworn he shook his head as if he were disappointed in me. I hated that. I closed the door and tried to forget the look in his eyes.

Inside, Melissa and Lucas were bouncing around the room. Does being in love give you more energy or something? I mean, I was *beat*. But the two of them looked all peppy and ready for anything.

"Let's play Scrabble!" said Melissa, rummaging around in her suitcase for her travel set.

"Oh, I don't know," I said. I was too tired to be able to think of good words.

"Sure, why not?" said Abby. I shot her a Look. She was just encouraging Melissa.

"Excellent!" Melissa cried, setting up the board on our coffee table. "Lucas and I can be one team and you guys can be the other."

Oh, sure. Abby and I were going to be great teammates. We were barely even speaking to each other.

Lucas saved the day. "No, let's split up," he said. "I want the chance to beat you." He smiled flirtatiously at Melissa. "Practice for tomorrow, you know."

For once, I drew some decent letters. That was a good thing, because I wasn't awake enough to be creative with my usual lineup. In fact, I went first, putting down the word *judge*. That was worth a good number of points.

I started to feel better. After all, Lucas and Melissa were sitting across from each other. It wasn't as if they were up to any kind of — *you* know. It was all totally innocent.

Lucas went next, putting down the word *quiet*.

"Ooh, good one." Melissa sighed. "It's so hard to use that Q."

"That's why I got rid of it right away," Lucas confessed. "It may not be good strategy, but at least I don't have to worry about it."

Abby didn't take long to slam down a decent word of her own: *taxi*.

"Whoa, the X," Lucas said, grinning.

"What am I going to do with that?" wailed Melissa. Then she sat up straight. "Ooh, I know!" She laid down three tiles to spell *oxen*.

"Excellent," said Lucas. "Hey, I have an idea. For the next round, let's all try to put down *slang* words or rude words. That's how my friends and I play sometimes."

"What do you mean?" I asked. "Like, 'butt'?"

Melissa giggled. Abby, believe it or not, blushed. But Lucas nodded. "Or snot, or fart. Words like that."

Now we were all giggling. And blushing a little. I looked down at my letters. "How about this?" I asked, putting down the word *nerd*.

Everybody cracked up. In fact, we were laughing so hard that I think we missed the first knock on the door. But we didn't miss the second. And we definitely didn't miss the sound of Mrs. Simon's voice calling, "Girls? Everything okay in there?"

Oh. My. Lord.

I clapped a hand over my mouth. Lucas jumped to his feet, looking around wildly. Melissa gave a little shriek. Abby was the only one to keep her head.

"Lucas," she hissed. "Into the closet."

Lucas gave her a wild-eyed stare. "Closet?" he repeated in a whisper, as if he had never heard the word before.

"Over there!" she hissed, pointing toward the door next to the bathroom. "Quick!"

"Girls?" Mrs. Simon knocked again.

"Coming!" sang out Abby. "Just a sec!"

Lucas finally began to move. He headed toward the closet and, quietly turning the doorknob, opened the door and let himself in. He closed the door behind him. Abby, on her way to let Mrs. Simon in, checked to make sure the closet door would stay shut. Then she strode to the hall door and flung it open. "Hi!" she said brightly.

"Hi," Mrs. Simon responded warily. "What's going on in here? I'm hearing a lot of noise from this room."

"We're just playing Scrabble," explained Abby, waving toward the board.

As Mrs. Simon turned her head to see, Melissa reached out — lightning-quick — to grab the tray that held Lucas's letters. *Yea, Melissa*, I thought.

"We're too keyed up to sleep," I said. My heart had finally calmed down a little and I could trust myself to speak again. "You know, because of the finals tomorrow."

"Well, that's understandable," Mrs. Simon said. "But to do your best, you need some sleep. I think you should finish up your game and hop into bed."

"Okay," Melissa said meekly. "You're probably right. In fact, I feel pretty tired all of a sudden." She gave a big stretch and a yawn.

Don't overact, I thought. But then I found myself yawning too. Fake or not, Melissa's yawn was contagious.

"All right, girls. I think you'll find you can sleep

now." Mrs. Simon smiled at us. "I want to wish you good luck for tomorrow. Whoever wins, I know you'll do SMS proud. You already have."

"Thank you," we chorused.

Finally, *finally* she left.

As the door closed behind her, the three of us threw ourselves on our beds. "Aaaaughhh!" Melissa squeaked. "That was *so* close."

The closet door opened a crack. "Can I come out now?" Lucas whispered.

"Wait a second," Abby hissed. "Just until we're sure she's gone."

We listened intently until we heard the sound of another door closing, down the hall.

"Okay," said Abby.

Lucas emerged from the closet, white as a sheet. "I'm out of here," he said. "That was scary. We could have gotten kicked out of the competition."

"And all for a nerd," I couldn't help saying. We started giggling again, but Abby shushed us.

Lucas left, and the three of us settled into our beds and turned out the lights. "That was actually kind of fun," Abby said into the dark.

"It was," I admitted. "I have to remember to thank Agent Melendez for not ratting us out."

"He's cool," Melissa said.

There was a good feeling in the room. Abby and I had actually managed to forget about the debates.

Until Melissa brought them up. "Good luck tomorrow, you guys," she whispered. "I'm going to come see which of you can convince me."

"It won't take much," Abby had to say. "I mean, you already know that dogs are cooler than cats, right?"

"Right," I said, feeling all my competitiveness rise up again. "But I don't want a *cool* pet. I want a *good* pet. And cats are the best."

Melissa sighed loudly. "I'm sorry I brought it up," she said. "Good night, you two."

"Good night," I answered. Abby just rolled over to face the wall. I lay there for a long time before I fell asleep, thinking that I could hardly wait until the finals were over.

❀ Chapter 12

I woke with a start the next morning, before our wake-up call came. I'd tossed and turned in the night, and every time I fell asleep I ended up dreaming about debates and debating. Mostly I dreamed about arguing with Abby, but some of the dreams were kind of weird. In one of them, a big golden retriever was standing at a podium, making point after point to his opponent, a Siamese cat.

Who won? Good question. Unfortunately, a fight broke out before the closing arguments were finished. The audience — all cats and dogs — began brawling.

That wasn't going to happen at *our* debate. No, we'd be civilized and proper. No scratching, no biting, no barking, no yowling. Just a war of words. Were my weapons ready? I wasn't sure. The only thing I was sure of was that I had a major case of butterflies in my stomach.

The finals were a big deal. Instead of taking place at the hotel, in one of the debate rooms, they were to be held at the Lincoln Memorial. We'd be onstage, not only in front of our peers, but in front of an audience drawn by the event, as well as any tourists who happened by. If that weren't enough to make me nervous, there was the building itself. It's an imposing place, with its gigantic columns (thirty-six of them, to symbolize the thirty-six states in the Union when Lincoln died) and the huge sculpture of Lincoln himself, so dignified and serious. The idea of his gaze on me while I debated was definitely intimidating.

I glanced at Abby, who was still sound asleep. Was she as nervous as I was? I doubted it. She seemed so confident, so sure of herself. Of course, it helped that she was on the "dog" side.

I went over the opening argument our team had worked out for the finals. I'd be our first debater that afternoon, and I wanted to be ready.

Cats, I said to myself, *are clean, self-sufficient animals. They are friendly. They are useful, when they catch mice. They are beautiful to look at and pleasant to stroke or hold.* All true. But kind of — weak. What if my opponent brought up the training issue?

Most dogs at least know how to sit and shake hands, lie down, and come when called. But what do cats know how to do? They're not so easy to train. Of course, I had to remember that if my opponent brought that up, I had a good rebuttal: *Cats are too intelligent to be bothered with learning silly tricks.*

Just then, the phone rang, jolting me fully awake. I jumped out of bed to answer it. It was our wake-up call. The day had officially begun.

Melissa and Abby stretched and yawned. I went to the window and pulled aside the curtain. "It's a beautiful day," I reported.

"Yahoo," said Abby, rolling over and putting her pillow over her head. "What time did we finally go to sleep?"

"I don't know," Melissa answered from her bed, "but I'm still tired."

I was too nervous to be tired. "What are you guys wearing today?" I asked, studying the three clean blouses I had left.

Melissa sat up in bed. "I packed a skirt," she told me. "I'll probably wear that, with a white blouse."

Melissa's finals were being held at the Lincoln Memorial too. All the finals would be there. We'd have a chance to see some of the advanced debaters at work before our turn came.

"I think I'll wear my bathrobe," Abby mumbled from beneath her pillow. "It's comfy and flattering, and after I'm done debating I can go right back to bed."

"Abby," I said, "come on. It's time to get up."

She moaned. "Oh, all right."

Ten minutes later, Abby popped out of the shower, wide awake and raring to go. "Aaah," she said, rubbing her hair with a towel, "that's more like it."

She didn't seem nervous at all.

Which was psyching me out.

I decided to dress as quickly as possible and find David and Kai for a Team DKK pep rally.

I found them having breakfast, sitting at a table with Mr. Hawthorne. I joined them, inviting Agent Melendez (my ever-present shadow) to sit with us as well. He turned me down, taking an unobtrusive seat nearby instead.

"We agents are used to sitting alone," Mr. Hawthorne told me. "Don't worry about him."

"I know," I said. "I'm just getting — kind of attached."

"I wish David had stayed a little more attached to Agent Sanford," he muttered with a little smile.

"Me too," I answered quietly, smiling back. "Oh,

well. It's only for another day. Then David will be safe at home."

Mr. Hawthorne nodded. "I'll be glad of it, and so will his mother."

"What are you guys mumbling about?" asked David as he buttered a piece of toast.

"Nothing!" I said brightly. "So, are we all ready?"

"Definitely," Kai answered. "We have this one in the bag."

David nodded. "Kai's right. We have nothing to worry about. We're going to trample the competition."

"Yeah!" I said, putting more enthusiasm into the word than I actually felt. "Right! Go, DKK!"

"You're nervous, aren't you?" asked David.

Oh, shoot. Was it that obvious?

I nodded.

"Don't be. We're a team, remember? We'll be together every step of the way."

"Just keep your head," Kai advised. "Remember, it's facts and figures. Let the evidence speak for itself."

I nodded again, as if they were convincing me. But my butterflies were still there, fluttering around the toast I'd just eaten.

My nerves never did go away. Instead, the nervous feeling just kept building as we walked to the Lincoln Memorial, found seats, and watched the advanced debaters go at it. They were amazing. They spoke so clearly and convincingly that I had no trouble following their arguments, even though the subject was way over my head. Would I ever be able to debate that well?

Before I knew it, our turn had come. After a quick three-way handshake for good luck, David, Kai, and I took our places on the stage. Abby and her teammates took theirs too. My eyes met hers as she positioned herself, and I felt a shiver run down my spine. Then one of the judges welcomed us and introduced us to the crowd. "These young people are just starting out in debate," he said. "But they've already impressed us with their skill." He turned to face us. "Good luck to all of you." Then he called for the first debaters to present their opening arguments.

The audience applauded. I felt as if I were in a dream, cut off from the real world. I stood and walked to the podium on our side of the stage.

Then a terrible thing happened.

Abby stood up too — and went to the podium on her team's side.

I hadn't pictured myself actually arguing against

Abby. I mean, I knew we were up against her team, but somehow I thought I'd be facing one of the others. Abby and I were *not* a good combination. We'd argued way too much over the last few days. As I watched her settle her notes on the podium, I knew it was going to be hard to keep a lid on my emotions.

And it was.

During my opening argument, I heard myself slipping into a tone of voice that was not even-tempered and cool. I sounded defensive and angry, but I couldn't help myself. This debate *was* personal. It had become that way over the last few days, whether I'd meant it to or not. "Even though *some* people can't admit it," I found myself saying, as I glared at Abby, "cats are smarter than dogs. In fact, cats are smarter than some people!" I gave Abby a meaningful glance.

Abby sounded just like me. Everything she said had this little *edge* to it. It wasn't a debate anymore. It was a fight.

Between my opening argument and our chance for rebuttal, David and Kai tried to calm me down. "You're not doing yourself any favors," David said. "That kind of emotion won't make the judges happy."

"Remember," put in Kai. "Stick to the evidence."

They helped me work on my rebuttal — we had five minutes to pull it together — and then I was facing Abby again. This time I was a little more polite, a little more relaxed. So was she. Her teammates must have given her the same speech mine gave me.

Finally, *finally* it was over. The audience applauded again, and Abby and I nodded at each other and sat down with our teams. I closed my eyes and took a long, deep breath. I glanced at Abby. She looked as relieved as I felt. Maybe now we could be in the same room without arguing. We'd had our debate, and there wasn't really any more to say. The judges would have the last word on who had won the debate. Of course I hoped they would choose my team, but no matter who won, I was glad to know that Abby and I wouldn't have to mention dogs or cats to each other ever again.

The judge who'd welcomed us stood up again. "Thank you, ladies and gentlemen," he said. "The judges will step away now to discuss the merits of your arguments. Please shake hands and be seated. We'll return shortly with a decision." He led the others toward a curtained area at the back of the stage.

Kai, David, and I stood up and walked toward

Abby's team for handshakes. As Abby and I shook, I happened to look over her shoulder, out into the audience.

I gasped.

A man was moving through the small crowd.

A man I recognized.

A man I feared.

Lance Dibdin had arrived.

❋ Chapter 13

I screamed.

And then I screamed again.

David whipped his head around to stare at me.

I couldn't speak. Instead, I just pointed at Dibdin.

Everything happened so fast after that that it's all a blur in my mind. But afterward, when we talked about it, we were able to reconstruct the scene.

Dibdin was moving fast, toward the stage and David. What was he going to do? Grab David then and there? Or did he have a weapon?

Mr. Hawthorne had one. A gun, that is. No question about it. He pulled it out from beneath his jacket in one smooth move, just the way they do in the movies. He was running as he did it — running toward Dibdin. He looked determined, serious, focused.

"Dad!" David gasped. His face had turned completely white. He looked wildly back at me. "Dibdin may be armed!" he said. He looked as if he might pass out.

Kai and I grabbed David and pulled him toward the curtained area, where the judges had gone.

"What — ?" David was staring back at the podium.

"Forget about it," I said, pushing him toward the curtain. "Just move!" He stumbled toward the curtain. Kai helped him find his way in as I turned back to check on Dibdin's location.

Total chaos met my eyes. The people in the audience were on their feet, milling around as they tried to figure out what was going on. Security guards in blue uniforms were running toward the stage. I couldn't see Agent Melendez, even though I knew he was out there. Mr. Hawthorne was working his way through the crowd, trying to get to Dibdin. And Dibdin was dodging between people, still heading toward the stage.

Those curtains wouldn't do much to protect David if Dibdin was armed.

I heard screams and shouting. Somebody cursed. A baby started to cry.

"What's going on?" Abby stared at me. "Is it that guy? The kidnapper?"

I nodded.

"What should we do?" She sounded panicky.

I shook my head. "I don't know. Stay out of the way, I guess." As far as I could tell, Dibdin wasn't coming toward me. Maybe he hadn't recognized me, or he didn't consider me important enough to bother with.

But I didn't feel safe, even knowing that Agent Melendez was somewhere nearby. I wouldn't, until Dibdin was caught. And so far, he was doing a good job of avoiding that. The security guards couldn't seem to get close to him. Mr. Hawthorne couldn't either.

Then I saw an opening in the crowd. Mr. Hawthorne saw it too. He gestured to Melendez, who had appeared out of nowhere. "This way!" he shouted. He plunged through the gap in the crowd toward Dibdin.

Our kidnapper didn't have a chance after that.

Later, I told David that his dad should consider switching careers. He could make a good living playing professional football, judging by the way he tackled Dibdin, bringing him down hard and fast.

Agent Melendez jumped on him too, grabbing Dibdin's arms and pulling them behind his back. He snapped on a pair of handcuffs faster than you could say "Busted!" and then began patting Dibdin down, looking for a weapon.

Several security guards arrived at the spot within moments. Mr. Hawthorne spoke to them quickly, and they fanned out again. Did Mr. Hawthorne think Dibdin had accomplices? (I found out later that he suspected it, but the guards didn't find anyone suspicious.)

The people in the audience were still milling around, unsure of what was going on. As I said, it all happened fast. Some of them probably hadn't even seen Dibdin, or noticed Mr. Hawthorne's drawn gun, or witnessed the flying tackle.

Once Dibdin was subdued, Mr. Hawthorne stood up and raised his hands. "Okay, everyone, you can take your seats and settle down. There's no reason to be alarmed. We have everything under control."

Slowly, people began to return to their seats. A security guard helped Dibdin to his feet and began to march him toward the nearest exit.

Before he left the building, Dibdin turned and stared into my eyes. The look he gave me was intense. I bet I'll have nightmares about it. There was no question anymore: He recognized me.

Mr. Hawthorne hurried up to the podium. "Are you okay, Kristy?" he asked, taking me by the elbows and looking into my face.

"I'm fine," I said. "David's back there." I waved toward the curtain.

"I know. I saw you push him out of the way. You have excellent reflexes, Kristy. I can't thank you enough. If Dibdin had been armed — "

"He wasn't, though, right?"

Mr. Hawthorne shook his head. "Fortunately, no. I hate to think what might have happened if he had been."

Just then, David and the judges came out from behind the curtain.

"Dad!" David ran toward his father. "Are you all right?"

Mr. Hawthorne reached out and drew David close for a hug. "I'm fine, son. And Dibdin won't be bothering you anymore."

I saw David take a huge, deep breath, and I had a feeling he was struggling to keep from crying.

"It's okay, David," I said, patting his back.

He stepped away from his dad. "You saved me again, Kristy," he said shakily. "Thanks."

"Kai helped," I said, shrugging.

"Son, I need to do some follow-up on this. Are you okay?" Mr. Hawthorne gave David a serious look.

"I'll be fine." David managed a smile.

"By the way," Mr. Hawthorne added, "you were terrific in your debate. All of you were."

The debate! I'd nearly forgotten. But nobody else had. I realized that the judges had taken their places again, and that the audience had settled down. Mr. Hawthorne realized it too. He gave David one last quick squeeze and headed off the stage.

David, Kai, and I took our seats. Abby and her teammates were already seated.

Everything seemed unreal. Did I even care anymore who had won the debate?

Actually, I did.

The judge who'd been acting as spokesperson stood up and faced the audience. "First, I'd like to thank you all for your patience and for keeping calm during this unexpected incident — an incident, I might add, that has ended happily."

There was a sprinkling of applause. I glanced at David. He still looked dazed.

"Second," continued the judge, "the time has come for us to announce our decision. We were able to reach one despite the interruption." He turned to face us, the debaters. "We're pleased to award first prize to the team of David Hawthorne, Kristy Thomas, and Kai Teh Tao."

I heard applause. I spotted Agent Melendez in the front row, clapping. He was — believe it or not — smiling! I was pleased that he'd stayed to find out who won. Abby's team applauded for us too. I checked her face and had the feeling she was honestly happy for me. The judge handed us each a small trophy, shaking our hands in turn.

"We also have a prize for the tournament's best overall debater in this category. That prize goes to Kai Teh Tao."

This time, David and I joined in the applause. "Yes!" I cried.

Kai was blushing as he accepted another trophy from the judge, but I could tell he was pleased.

"A complete report on our judging process will be available later today," the judge informed us. "But I will mention one factor that influenced our decision, since I think it may be of general interest and may serve as a lesson to other beginning debaters."

He glanced sternly at me and then at Abby. "The

judges were not pleased to see signs of personal conflict during the debate. But we *were* happy to see that the two debaters in question were able to switch gears, presumably with the help and advice of their teammates, and finish off their debate in a civil and dignified manner. We hope they've learned from this experience."

My eyes met Abby's. We smiled as the crowd applauded some more. As we filed off stage, I gave Agent Melendez a little wave. This was probably good-bye. I wouldn't see him again now that Dibdin had been caught. He waved back, giving me a thumbs-up and a broad smile. In a funny way, I was going to miss Agent Melendez.

Abby and I walked back to the hotel together. We weren't talking, but I had a feeling we were thinking the same thing. The judge's remarks had been prompted by the public debate we'd just been through. But they also applied to our friendship. We had let arguing get in the way of enjoying each other's company. We had some talking to do — but I knew we could work things out.

❋ Chapter 14

I reached under the bed and came up with two mismatched dirty socks. Abby and I were in our room, packing. The convention was officially over, and in a few hours we'd be climbing onto the bus for the trip home. Meanwhile, it was time to round up everything I'd brought and try to stuff it back into my overnight bag.

It was also time for Abby and me to clear the air — but I didn't know how to begin. I kept glancing at her, and a couple of times I caught her looking back at me. I wondered if she was thinking the same thing I was. If so, I wished she'd bring it up, so I wouldn't have to.

I've never been good at this sort of thing. It's Mary Anne's specialty, not mine. But frankly, the silence was beginning to drive me nuts. We had hardly spoken since we'd left the Lincoln Memorial. Oh, Abby had congratulated me and the rest of my team on our win, and I'd said all the right things about how both teams had been great and her team could have won just as easily. Which was true. I was impressed that Abby and I had made it to the finals in the first place. I was pretty sure we were going to stick with debating after this. Maybe we'd be back at another convention next year, debating at the next level. If so, I hoped we could at least be on the same team. That way, we wouldn't have to argue all the time.

I reached under my pillow to find my pj's. "So," Abby began.

"Yes?" I said eagerly.

"So that was wild, when David's father tackled that guy," she said lamely.

I had a feeling that was *not* what she'd intended to say. We'd already talked about what had happened when Dibdin showed up.

"Yeah," I answered, stuffing my pj's into my bag. "And how about the way Agent Melendez snapped the handcuffs on him? It was just like in the cop shows."

"I know!" Abby was folding her skirt and laying it in her suitcase.

"Pretty cool," I mumbled.

"Definitely."

Then there was silence again. I couldn't take it.

"Abby," I said finally.

She looked at me. "What?"

"I — I was wondering if you packed your toothbrush. Don't forget it!"

"Oh — thanks," she said. "I almost did." She disappeared into the bathroom.

I looked at myself in the mirror over the bureau and rolled my eyes. Why was I being a chicken? Why was it such a big deal to have a talk with a friend?

I made a silly, scrunched-up face at myself, just as Abby came back into the room. She burst out laughing. "What are you doing?"

I turned to face her. "Just — Abby, we have to talk."

"I know. It's been — "

"This weekend — " We both started talking at once.

"You go," she said.

"No, you," I said.

We looked at each other and laughed nervously.

"Okay, I'll go," I said. The hard part had been getting started. Now maybe I could talk. "I guess I just want us to be friends again. I hated all that arguing. We have such similar personalities in some ways. We're both so competitive, and we always say just what we think."

"I know. It's tough sometimes, isn't it? We're both so stubborn. I mean, we're friends and all, but sometimes it's hard to remember that."

We looked down at the floor for a moment. "So, that's it?" I asked. "Now that the debate is over, we can quit arguing and go back to being friends?" I looked at her with a tentative smile.

She didn't smile back. In fact, she didn't even look up. She was still staring at the floor.

"Abby?"

Still she didn't look up.

"Abby, what's the matter?"

"It's just that . . ." She paused. "This weekend has been hard for me. I've been feeling left out."

"Left out? What do you mean? We've all been hanging around together."

"Not really," she said. Now she was looking at me. "You spent most of your time with David and Kai. And Melissa's been with Lucas."

"But you had *your* team," I said, confused.

She shook her head. "But we weren't friends," she said. "We never really clicked that way. We were only together when we needed to practice."

"Wow." Abby had really been hurting. It had never even occurred to me that I'd been ignoring her, but now I could see that I hadn't paid her much attention. I'd been too caught up with David, and with practicing. And when Abby and I *had* been together, we'd spent every minute arguing. "I'm sorry, Abby. Really, I am."

"I kept hoping this trip would be a good chance for us to hang out. You know, just you and me."

"Yeah. I blew it, didn't I?"

She gave me a tiny smile. "Kind of."

"Well, I'm sorry," I said again. "That was dumb. I just didn't see what I was doing. I mean, I definitely noticed that we were arguing a lot. But, well, I'm glad you told me." I was too. My friends are very important to me.

"Me too." Abby bent over to zip up her suitcase. "So, that's that. Can we go back to normal now?"

"Sure," I said. "Except I have one confession to make."

"What's that?"

"I was jealous of you," I admitted.

"Why?" She looked surprised.

"Because you had the good side in the debate. The right side. I just kept wishing I was on that side."

She stared at me. "You're kidding."

I shook my head.

She cracked up.

"What?"

"Guess what?" she replied. "I kept wishing I had *your* side."

"Get out of here. Why?"

"Because it was right."

"How can you *say* that?" I could hardly believe my ears.

"Because it's true! Dogs are slobbery, dumb beasts. Cats are elegant, intelligent animals." Abby folded her arms and grinned at me.

"Are you out of your mind? Dogs may be slobbery, but at least they don't cough up hairballs."

"A few hairballs are a small price to pay for an animal that's clean and quiet and can take care of itself. You don't have to walk a cat three times a day, you know," she answered.

We were facing each other across the room, just as if we were in front of an audience at a debate. It all felt very familiar, except that we had switched sides.

"I know, I know." I moaned. "I made that point about ten times over this weekend. But I didn't believe a word of it. I was just thinking about how much better dogs are. I mean, you can't wrestle with a cat! You can't play fetch with a cat or take it swimming!"

"So?" said Abby. "You can't hold a dog on your lap and pet it until it purrs. And dogs don't catch mice."

"Some do," I protested. "My aunt used to have a dog that caught mice. It would pounce on them out in the field behind her house."

"Okay, so maybe one dog can catch mice," Abby said. "But you have to admit most of them are good for nothing."

"Never!" I cried. "I'll never admit that!"

We stared at each other for a second — and then cracked up.

"Can you believe what we're doing?" asked Abby, throwing herself down on the bed.

I was laughing so hard my stomach hurt. "We can't seem to stop. It's just in our nature to argue."

"Like cats and dogs!" Abby managed to squeak out. That cracked us up all over again.

Just then, there was a knock at the door.

"Who could that be?" I asked Abby.

"Maybe Melissa forgot her key," Abby said. Melissa had gone off with Lucas for one last romantic walk along the Mall.

I went to the door. "Who is it?" I asked.

"David."

"And his dad," added a deeper voice.

I checked in the peephole, then opened the door. David and Mr. Hawthorne were standing there, smiling. "Hi!" I said. "Come on in."

"What's going on in here?" David asked. "What's so funny? We could hear you laughing from all the way down the hall."

Abby and I looked at each other. "It's a long story," I said. We giggled a little.

"Whatever," David said. "Listen, when do you guys have to leave?"

I checked my watch. "In about three hours."

"Are you all packed and everything?"

"Just about," Abby answered. "Why?"

"Because we'd like to take you somewhere special," said David. He looked at his dad and smiled. "Dad wants to give you a tour of his office."

That didn't sound very exciting, but I didn't want to be rude. "Sure," I said. "That sounds very interesting."

"Thank you, Mr. Hawthorne," said Abby politely. "Do we have to wear nicer clothes, though?" We'd already changed into T-shirts and jeans.

"No, you both look just fine," he told her. "Well?

Are you ready to go? We've already checked with Mrs. Simon, and she says it's fine."

"You'll like this," David promised.

I wasn't so sure. Touring an office wasn't my idea of a thrilling way to spend the last hours of my time in Washington. But what could I say? We left a note for Melissa and followed David and Mr. Hawthorne downstairs.

✺ Chapter 15

"Wait a minute," I said as the black car we were riding in pulled up to a door guarded by men in uniform. "I thought we were going to your office."

"Mmm-hmm," said Mr. Hawthorne. "We are. My office is in this building."

"But — " Abby managed to say. Her mouth was hanging open.

Mine was too. "But this is the White House!" I finally said. We'd driven around to a side door, but there was no mistaking the building for anything else.

"Where the President lives," Abby added, as if we all didn't know that.

"That's right!" Mr. Hawthorne said cheerily.

I looked at David with narrowed eyes. "You never told me — " I began.

He grinned and shrugged. "You never asked," he replied.

I gave him a little punch in the arm. "But this is so *cool*!"

"You don't even know how cool it is," David told me as we climbed out of the car and headed for the door. "My dad has an all-access pass," he whispered to Abby and me.

"Whoa!" said Abby.

"What does that mean?" I asked.

"I don't know," she admitted with a grin. "But it sounds impressive."

"It means he can go almost anywhere in the White House," David told us. "And he can take us almost anywhere too."

I was speechless.

"You're not going to get the usual tour," David promised. "Believe me, you'll remember this."

Mr. Hawthorne had been talking to the guards. Now he turned to us. "Do you girls have some ID on you?" he asked.

I checked the fanny pack I'd been wearing when I walked around the city. Inside was my wallet. I fished around for my SMS photo ID card. "Will this do?" I asked, holding it up.

He took it and examined it carefully. "A passport

would be better," he said seriously. "But I think this will work."

"I have mine too," said Abby, handing it to him.

He showed the IDs to the guard, who examined them even more carefully, then entered our names on his clipboard.

Mr. Hawthorne gave us an apologetic look. "I'm afraid I'll have to ask you to leave your bags here," he said. "Visitors have to check everything. But they'll be safe, I can guarantee that."

"No problem," I said. I handed over my fanny pack and Abby gave him her backpack. He passed them to the guard. Then the guard handed him something.

"I think we're set," said Mr. Hawthorne. He showed us what the guard had given him: two laminated passes with clips attached. GUEST, they read.

David already had a pass. And Mr. Hawthorne had one too, I now saw. His was clipped to his jacket. It looked a lot more official than ours did. But I'm not complaining! Ours were extremely cool.

I clipped mine to my shirt, and Abby did the same.

As I was wondering what would happen next, I heard Mr. Hawthorne call a greeting to someone. I looked up to see a man in uniform ride by on a bike, waving as he passed us.

"Whoa, cool!" said Abby.

"Isn't it?" asked Mr. Hawthorne. "That's Agent Brancusi. He's one of our newest bike patrol agents. They patrol the White House compound. If they see anyone suspicious they can chase him — or her — down easily."

"Where do I sign up?" asked Abby. "Sounds like an excellent job."

"We'll keep you in mind," said Mr. Hawthorne, smiling. "Now, let's head inside, shall we? You'll just need to walk through this metal detector."

"Is that in case we're carrying weapons?" I asked.

He nodded seriously. "We don't take any chances," he said. "There are detectors at every entrance. Everyone has to go through them."

We walked through without causing any beeping, and Mr. Hawthorne led us down a long hallway. We passed doors on each side, which he told us led to offices for White House staff. "I thought you might like to see the briefing room," he said, "where the President holds press conferences."

"I've seen that on TV," I said. "Do you think there's one going on now?"

He checked his watch. "There might be. But the President probably won't be speaking. There's often a briefing at this time by White House staff."

Sure enough, when we peeked into the room, a crowd of reporters was listening to a man who was standing at a podium in front of a blue curtain. The man was answering a question, while a handful of reporters took notes.

"But it's so small," said Abby. "I've seen it on TV too, and I always thought it was this big, grand room."

David laughed. "You should see it when there's something major happening and the President is speaking. All the reporters try to get the President's attention by yelling and waving. It's wild."

We watched for awhile. Then Mr. Hawthorne suggested we might like to see some of the places on the regular tour, such as the Blue Room.

"I'd rather see the inside stuff," I confessed. "I can come back for a regular tour some other time."

Abby agreed.

"Okay, then," said Mr. Hawthorne. "How about if we check out the kitchens?" He led us through a maze of hallways and into an elevator. When we'd gone down a floor or two, he led us through some more hallways until we entered the biggest kitchen

I've ever seen. At least twenty people were at work, all wearing white uniforms. A man in a suit was talking to one of them.

"That's the White House butler," Mr. Hawthorne whispered. "He's probably talking to the chef about an upcoming dinner. They have to do a lot of planning when the President is having two hundred good friends over for dinner. Especially if one of them happens to be a king or something."

"I'd be too nervous to cook for a king," I said. "Imagine if you burned the casserole!"

"These chefs are professionals," Mr. Hawthorne replied. "But I bet they get nervous too sometimes."

Just then, he put a hand to his ear, the one the wire went to. Then he spoke into his sleeve for a few seconds. "Oops," he told us. "I have to leave you for a few minutes. Not an emergency, but something I have to deal with."

"Do we have to leave?" Abby asked.

Mr. Hawthorne shook his head. "David can take care of you," he said. "We can meet up again in, say, twenty minutes? In my office?"

"Sure," David said.

Mr. Hawthorne took off. David turned to us with a grin. "Okay," he said. "Time for one of my favorite activities."

"What's that?" I asked.

"Find Sparky."

"You mean, the President's cat?" Abby said, staring at him. Everybody's seen that cat on TV. It was hard to believe David had seen him in real life.

"Yup," said David. "He likes to hang out down here, or even further downstairs, in the basement. I've found him in the strangest places."

"What are we waiting for?" I asked. "Let's go."

David led us all over that building. It was so cool. We saw some of the private rooms where the President and his family entertain guests. We saw more of the kitchens. We saw the woodshop, the repair shop, and the office that handles the heating and cooling of the White House — where there's a computer that shows the exact temperature in every single room!

We saw all kinds of people at work: people who were cleaning and cooking, polishing silver, moving furniture, or carrying stacks of papers from one place to another. Everyone seemed busy and in a hurry. It takes a lot of work to keep a place like the White House running.

We never did find Sparky, though Abby swore she saw a flash of white (he's white with black spots) when we were near the woodshop. But I didn't care. It was still the most awesome White House tour ever.

Finally, David led us back up to the offices where his dad is based. He showed us another really cool computer, one that monitors the exact location of every member of the President's family at all times. "That's one way they keep track," he explained.

David was lucky. I could see it wasn't easy for him to have a dad in the Secret Service, but there were some awesome perks!

We thanked Mr. Hawthorne for the tour and headed back to the hotel to catch our bus home. David came along to see us off.

"I'll visit you in Stoneybrook one of these days," he promised as we stood waiting to board our bus.

"You better," I told him. "I know Stacey would be happy if you did too."

Melissa and Lucas were off to one side, kissing and whispering and looking like sad little puppy dogs as they said their good-byes. "I'll miss you so much, Lukie," I heard Melissa say.

"And I'll miss you," said Lucas.

"I want you to have this," Melissa said, handing something to Lucas.

He laughed. "Your trophy! The one you earned

by beating me. I'll treasure it." He held the trophy to his chest. "Thank you," he said.

"You're welcome," said Melissa, smiling at me over his shoulder as she hugged him again.

I had a feeling Melissa would be back in D.C. soon. Maybe Abby and I would come with her. Washington had turned out to be a pretty exciting place to visit, and now I had friends there too. David, Mr. Hawthorne — and, of course, Agent Melendez.

L. GODWIN

Ann M. Martin

About the Author

ANN MATTHEWS MARTIN was born on August 12, 1955. She grew up in Princeton, NJ, with her parents and her younger sister, Jane.

Although Ann used to be a teacher and then an editor of children's books, she's now a full-time writer. She gets ideas for her books from many different places. Some are based on personal experiences. Others are based on childhood memories and feelings. Many are written about contemporary problems or events.

All of Ann's characters, even the members of the Baby-sitters Club, are made up. (So is Stoneybrook.) But many of her characters are based on real people. Sometimes Ann names her characters after people she knows; other times she chooses names she likes.

In addition to the Baby-sitters Club books, Ann Martin has written many other books for children. Her favorite is *Ten Kids, No Pets* because she loves big families and she loves animals. Her favorite BSC book is *Kristy's Big Day.* (Kristy is her favorite baby-sitter.)

Ann M. Martin now lives in New York with her cats, Gussie, Woody, and Willy, and her dog, Sadie. Her hobbies are reading, sewing, and needlework — especially making clothes for children.

Look for #10

STACEY'S PROBLEM

My rollerblades were way in the back. As I pulled them free of the other stuff, I heard Dad and Samantha talking softly in the living room.

Why were they being so quiet, as if they didn't want me to hear what they were saying? I strained to listen, but I couldn't make out their words.

"I'm ready!" I called, heading out of my room. Dad took the blades Samantha had given him for his birthday from the box under the couch, and we all headed out for Central Park.

We had a great time, skating along the park paths, though it might have been better if we hadn't had to keep slowing down for Dad to catch up. He's not too swift on his wheels yet. (Despite Samantha's warning, we did wait for him.)

Dad said we were going out to dinner later, so we just caught a quick snack from a vendor. I love the potato knishes they sell. Dad and Samantha ate hot dogs with sauerkraut while the three of us sat together on a bench beside a path.

Dad suddenly turned to Samantha. "I hope you don't mind, but I just can't wait until dinner tonight to tell her," he said.

"All right," Samantha agreed happily. "Tell her now."

"Tell me what?" I asked.

Part of me already knew what he was going to say.

Check out what's new with your old friends.